If You Scrooge, You Lose

Written By

Constance Holden

www.rdtalleybooks.com

Las Vegas, Nevada

ISBN: 978-1-957294-12-4 (paperback)

R.D. Talley Books Publishing, LLC
The Forum Shops at Caesars Palace
3500 Las Vegas Blvd. South, Suite T17
Las Vegas, Nevada 89109
www.rdtalleybooks.com

Dedication

To every woman who chose herself first and feared she lost everything in doing so.

To every man who loved with patience, not pressure.

And to every couple who had to find their rhythm a second time. This is your reminder: love delayed is not love denied.

Contents

Introduction

Some love stories don't start with fireworks. Some begin in the quiet places—right before the mistake, the missed moment, or the heartbreaking goodbye. And sometimes, they don't truly begin until you've lived enough life to know what you almost lost.

If You Scrooge, You Lose is a story about timing, ambition, pride, and the delicate art of letting love back in. It's about the choices we make in pursuit of success— and what happens when the heart we left behind shows up again, not as a ghost from the past, but as a possibility for the future. This is for the ones who were too focused, too afraid, or too heartbroken the first time around. This is for the second chance that didn't knock—it broke down the door.

There's a certain magic that comes around only once a year. It flickers in twinkling lights, simmers in slow-cooked family recipes, and lingers in laughter echoing through cozy rooms. But for some—especially those of us wired for hustle—it's all too easy to miss.

We live in a world that praises productivity and applauds the grind. For workaholics, even Christmas can start to feel like just another item on the to-do list. But here's the truth: when you choose work over wonder, hustle over heart, and deadlines over December joy… *you lose.*

You lose the chance to slow down and savor the moments that matter. You lose the sweetness of shared memories, spontaneous laughter, warm embraces, and the quiet kind of peace that only the holidays bring.

If You Scrooge, You Lose is more than a clever phrase—it's a heartfelt reminder that love, connection, and presence are worth more than any paycheck or project. It's about reclaiming the season, even if just for a few magical moments, to be present, to be joyful, and to let love lead.

This story is a celebration of second chances, rekindled romance, and the courage it takes to choose the heart over the hustle. It also means don't hesitate—or overthink, or let fear win, or hold back from love out of pride, pain, or poor timing. So, if you've ever found yourself missing the magic because of the grind, if you've ever been afraid to love again, or wondered if it's too late to say yes to something real—this book is for you.

1

The Grind Never Stops

Renee Carrington sat in her sleek, modern office at 9:07 PM, finishing the final touches on her Q4 sales projection report that was due first thing Monday morning after Christmas. Her head heavily buzzed from caffeine, her phone rang with unanswered calls and text messages from her mother and family members, and somewhere deep in her gut, she felt the hollow ache of isolation she'd long trained herself to ignore.

Renee was 35 years old, VP of Sales at Foster and Sanders, and by anyone's standard, she was killing it. She lived for this; the promotions, the accolades, the envy of peers who couldn't keep up. What she didn't live for were Friday family dinners, birthday parties, or Sunday brunch with her college friends. *Work pays the bills. Sentimentality doesn't,* she often told herself, as if it were scripture.

Her personal assistant, and only friend she'd let get close to her, Lila Thompson, poked her head into the office with an amused expression on her face.

"Boss lady, it's getting late. Shouldn't you be heading home?"

"Home for what?" Renee scoffed, her fingers flying over the keyboard. "Netflix and silence?" she added, not glancing up from the glowing screen filled with contracts and Q4 projections.

Lila chuckled and stepped into the corner office, arms behind her back, practically bouncing in her ballet flats. She looked like Christmas morning wrapped in a cable-knit sweater and a peppermint-scented aura. "I just came to say goodbye before heading out. I'll be gone until after New Year's, remember?"

Renee finally looked up, blinking at her assistant as if she were a calendar reminder she'd ignored too many times. "Right. Your annual 'Hot Cocoa & Hibernation' escape with the girls. Vermont, isn't it?"

"Snowshoeing, sleigh rides, sappy movies, matching pajamas—the whole cliché," Lila beamed. "But before I go…" She pulled a small, square box from behind her back and placed it on Renee's desk. The wrapping was homemade—brown craft paper decorated with tiny pine trees, hand-stamped in green and gold. Tied with twine and a cinnamon stick, it looked like something plucked from a nostalgic holiday magazine.

"I made it during our girls' night ornament swap. I drew your name. Technically, you were supposed to be there… again."

Renee smirked. "Yes, well, I was busy saving a client from a lawsuit and myself from a lawsuit over a missed gala. But I do appreciate the gesture." She untied the twine with practiced grace and opened the box. Inside was a hand-painted ceramic ornament. It featured a miniature version of her high-rise skyline view, with tiny snowflakes and the words, *Even bosses need a little magic.* Renee's breath hitched. It was…charming. Intimate. Thoughtful. Not bought, not branded. Just made. And it glistened with sincerity.

"Lila, I…" Her voice faltered, just slightly. "This is…unexpected." Lila shrugged, trying to play it cool.

"We all put our hearts into them. Figured you could use a little sparkle on that tree you keep threatening to buy but never do."

For a moment, silence settled between them— comfortable for Lila, a little suffocating for Renee. The ornament sat in her palm like a reminder of something she couldn't quite name. Or had tried hard to forget.

Then Renee cleared her throat and slid a sleek white envelope across the desk.

"This is for you. First-class round trip anywhere in the world. Doesn't expire. You've earned it."

Lila's eyes widened. "Renee! This is…wow. Are you serious?"

"Completely. You work miracles with my schedule and haven't taken a real vacation in three years. Call it an investment into your sanity."

"Thank you." Lila's voice softened. "But for the record, no trip beats a night with the girls. Glitter, glue guns, and that terrible mulled wine we keep making just because it's tradition."

Renee chuckled despite herself, but the laugh faded quickly. Lila's words hit deeper than intended. She hadn't attended a girls' night in over three years. She hadn't had a spontaneous moment that didn't involve legal strategy or profit margins. When had she last laughed until her mascara smudged?

The ornament sat on her desk, twinkling gently under the office lights. Lila gave her a quick hug—one Renee pretended to be too stiff to accept but didn't pull away from. Lila sighed, trying again.

"Didn't your family beg-invite you to the family cabin in Asheville this weekend?"

"Hard pass," Renee muttered, sarcastically.

Lila shook her head, mumbling, *"Suit yourself, Scrooge."* Renee didn't hear her—or pretended not to. She couldn't care less about gingerbread houses or fireside laughs. Her family didn't understand. She wasn't about *fun*. She was about *winning*.

"Merry Christmas, boss lady," Lila said, slipping out the door with one last twinkle-eyed smile.

Renee looked at the ornament again. Then at her inbox. Then back at the ornament. The cursor blinked. The numbers waited. But something small and warm stirred in her chest—like the echo of a carol she used to know by heart.

The Ones She Missed

After Lila left, Renee sat motionless, the ornament still cradled in her palm. The skyline painted on it shimmered softly, but in her mind, it began to blur— replaced by another memory entirely.

It was the year she broke things off with David Bennett. The breakup was swift and surgical. No drawn-out fights, no reconciliation dinners, no second guesses. He had wanted a family. Balance. Holidays that didn't come with a corporate strategy. Renee wanted armor. David peeled it off too easily, and she didn't like how exposed she felt.

That Friday, after David said goodbye, her phone buzzed with a group text from three of her college friends: *Paint and Sip Night! Girls Only. Bring your broken hearts and your favorite bottle of whatever!* They sent photos from the event later—paint-smudged hands, goofy grins, mismatched aprons. One canvas had "Breakups Build Baddies" scrawled in neon across a sunset. Another had painted a wine glass with boxing gloves. Laughter practically echoed through the screen. They had saved her a seat. She never replied.

A year later, she missed Charmaine's baby shower. Claimed she was stuck at a corporate retreat in Aspen. Truth was, she just didn't want to explain why she was still single. The invitation glittered with little pastel onesies and said *"She's Having a Girl!"* in gold foil. She meant to send a gift but forgot.

And the gospel brunch? That one stung the most. Nina, her old roommate turned mimosa-sipping Sunday soul sister, had rented a rooftop with live music, chicken and waffles, and bottomless grace. *"Let's praise Him, then pass the syrup!"* the invite had said. Everyone wore shades of cream and coral. Renee said she had a flight to L.A. She didn't. She just couldn't stand to be reminded of the joy she no longer knew how to participate in. She hadn't seen Nina since.

Now, in the quiet of her office, surrounded by steel, glass and the hollow hum of success, Renee realized she hadn't just lost a boyfriend. She'd forfeited something bigger. Something warmer. Something real. Her eyes flicked to the ceramic ornament again. *Even bosses need a little magic.* She swallowed hard. Not yet ready to cry— but dangerously close.

One thing for certain, Renee Carrington had worked harder than anyone else at Foster and Sanders. Harder than the men who were automatically assumed to be leaders, harder than her colleagues who coasted on connections or generational privilege. She was the first and only Black female vice president in the company's 60-year history, a detail often whispered in conference rooms but never acknowledged outright.

It had taken her ten years of sacrifice, grit, and relentless determination to climb to this peak. No help from anyone else. She did this with her own hard work, sweat and tears. She remembered her first day like it was yesterday; one of only a handful of women in the boardroom and the *only* Black woman. It was a room where every move, every word, felt scrutinized under an invisible microscope. *"You'll have to work twice as hard,"* her mother had warned her back when she was just a girl, and she had.

At Foster and Sanders, "good enough" didn't apply to her. Excellence was the only option. She earned an MBA at the prestigious Duke University School of Business while balancing a full-time job, working late nights and weekends while her peers lived their carefree 20s. After graduation, when she was finally hired as a Senior Sales Manager at Foster and Sanders, she poured everything into proving herself. Her weekends disappeared. So did her nights. Sunday brunch with her sorority sisters became a distant memory; a photo album of smiling faces she never saw anymore. *"Where've you been, girl?"* they'd ask in texts she'd skim and never reply to.

Her friends had always been her backbone, especially her "girls' night" crew, women who knew her personal struggles and her dreams. They'd been the ones cheering her on, sipping cocktails and mocktails while sharing wild stories of their dating lives. Renee would sometimes joke about being married to her job, but over time, the joke stopped being funny. Her best friends had started getting engaged, married, and having babies. Invitations kept coming, but she declined one after another until they stopped altogether. Renee told herself it was worth it.

When David Bennett proposed to her five years ago, she had felt a moment of hesitation, like a small voice in her gut trying to pull her back from the edge of her relentless ambition. David was solid, loving, and patient. He'd held her hand, staring into her eyes, and asked her to marry him, to build a life together. *"Renee,"* he'd said softly, *"I know how much you love your work. But you can't build a future alone."* And yet, she'd chosen. She smiled regretfully, a lump in her throat she couldn't swallow, and told him she wasn't ready by not saying yes. *"I just got offered the VP promotion. This is my shot, David. I can't let it slip away. It wouldn't be fair to you to work late nights and I can't give you children right now."* He didn't argue. David wasn't that kind of man. He only nodded, disappointment flickering in his eyes. *"I hope you find what you're looking for, Renee."*

But has she found it?

Five Years Ago

The lights in the garden twinkled like tiny stars strung between the branches. The air buzzed with music, laughter, and the clinking of glasses as friends gathered under a warm summer sky to celebrate Renee and David's five-year couple anniversary. It was a night David had planned meticulously—every detail tailored to reflect their journey together. From the framed photo timeline hanging near the cake table, to the jazz playlist softly weaving through the air—it was all *them*. He had even told her best friend Monique to have her camera ready, just in case.

The ring burned a hole in his pocket. David stood off to the side of the patio, swirling a glass of champagne, watching Renee glide across the space like the star of her own show. Her smile was radiant, her laugh easy, and her eyes—when they met his—still had that light that first drew him in. But something about tonight felt different. He checked the time. Almost midnight. He'd waited until most guests were tipsy on wine and nostalgia. He wanted a quiet moment—just loud enough for her to hear his heart when he asked the question.

He moved to go find her, but just as he reached the open sliding doors, he heard her voice echo from the kitchen. The door was cracked, and he paused, about to knock.

"I still can't believe it," she was saying to Monique and Tasha, her voice breathless with excitement. "They finally promoted me to VP! They're flying me out to London next month to start training for one year. I didn't think it would happen so fast!"

"Girl! London? You're going global now!", Monique squealed with excitement.

"I know, right?!" Renee said, laughing. "It's everything I've worked for. And it's just getting started. I can't let anything—*or anyone*—slow me down right now."

There was a beat of silence before Tasha asked gently, "Even David?" David froze.

"Oh, come on, Tash," Renee replied, brushing it off with a nervous chuckle. "I love him, but we both know he's more of the settle-down-and-buy-a-house and pump-me full-of-babies type. And I'm still climbing, girl."

The rest of the conversation faded into white noise. David stepped back like he'd been shoved. The ring—once heavy with promise—suddenly felt hollow in his hand.

He waited until the party cleared out. Guests hugged them goodbye. Laughter drifted into the night. Renee was glowing from the compliments, from the wine, from the thrill of the promotion. And still, he couldn't stop himself…

As the last friend waved and the door closed, David reached into his pocket and knelt down in the middle of the quiet living room, surrounded by wilting balloons and flickering candles. Renee froze. Her eyes widened. "David…what are you doing?"
"I was going to do this earlier. But I didn't want to compete with the champagne and speeches," he said softly. "I thought I'd ask you something simple, now that it's just us." He opened the box. Her hands flew to her mouth, but she didn't say anything.

"Renee Elise Carrington," he said, forcing a smile. "Will you marry me?"

The silence that followed wasn't long. But it was loud.

"I—David…"

He stood before she could finish. "I already know," he said quietly, slipping the box shut and sitting it on the cocktail table. "Congratulations on the promotion." Then he kissed her on the forehead, as gently as if she were already a memory, and walked out of the house without looking back. That night, the ring went into a drawer. That chapter closed.

The VP promotion was hard-fought. Renee had overseen the biggest account in the firm's history, hitting numbers no one thought possible. She'd pulled all-nighters, skipped holidays, and powered through exhaustion while the other executives casually took family vacations. She navigated microaggressions with grace, endured being spoken over in meetings, and constantly had to "prove" that she deserved to be in the room. When the announcement came, it was almost anticlimactic.

"Congratulations, Renee," her boss had said with a handshake and a nod, as though she hadn't just bled for it. No fanfare. No celebration. Just a title. And yet, she told herself it was enough. Now, as Renee sat in her office, finishing a report while the city outside prepared for Christmas, she thought of all the moments she'd traded for her corner office: Brunches. Nights out. David. Laughing until her sides hurt. Friday dinners with her mom and siblings. All of it neatly set aside for *this*.

"Work pays the bills," she muttered to herself, her voice flat.

2

The Price of Perfection

Two days later, Renee sat alone as usual in her all-white immaculate high-rise condo with another take out meal. The only sounds were the soft hum of her refrigerator and an impersonal documentary on Netflix. Renee pulled her phone from the couch cushion and saw a dozen missed calls from Mom. She hovered her thumb over the callback button, but then stopped. *They'll just lecture me about being too busy.* Instead, Renee scrolled LinkedIn to admire her glowing professional reviews. Validation, neatly packaged. She didn't notice her mother's text: *"Renee, we miss you. This isn't healthy, baby. Call me."*

The next evening, alone once again, Renee set the cardboard takeout box on her spotless glass dining table, a glamorous dining set she almost never used. The condo around her was pristine…*too* pristine. The floors gleamed without a speck of dust, the granite counters reflected the sterile glow of the recessed lighting, and the white leather furniture sat perfectly staged, like a model home awaiting a showing. But Renee wasn't staging anything. This was her life.

She stabbed her fork into lukewarm lo mein, not bothering to plate it. The faint hum of her refrigerator was the only sound, interrupted occasionally by the ping of her phone as notifications rolled in:

Mom: *"Renee, baby, you coming to the cabin? Your cousins are here already, and we're all waiting for you."*

Mom: *"I made your favorite—sweet potato pie! Call me, please."*

Mom: *"Renee?"*

Renee placed the phone face down onto the table, as if ignoring it would make the messages stop. She took another bite, chewing slowly. The noodles tasted like the cardboard container they came in. Outside her large picture window, snow fell quietly over the city skyline. Cars rolled along the streets below, their headlights casting brief streaks of light on her walls. It was all so quiet—*too* quiet. She glanced up at the framed photograph on the counter, a relic from years ago. Her father's warm smile stared back at her, his arm slung lovingly around her mother and siblings on a past Christmas morning.

Renee remembered that day clearly—the smell of pine from the real tree, her mom's laughter, and her father humming Christmas carols as he carved the turkey. Her chest tightened. She pushed the box of lo mein aside, suddenly no longer hungry. Renee had no tree and hadn't put up any Christmas decorations in the past five years. The condo was a symbol of her success: minimalist, high-end, expensive. But suddenly it felt more like a museum than a home—a place where she *lived* but didn't *belong.*

Belong. The word rolled bitterly through her mind. Renee stood abruptly and paced to her desk, grabbing her laptop. Maybe work would drown out the silence. She powered it on, the glow of the screen lighting up her perfectly made-up face and clicked open a spreadsheet she'd already triple-checked. The cursor blinked at her, expectant, but her mind couldn't focus. Her phone pinged again. She ignored it. Again. With an irritated sigh, she picked it up and saw the latest text.

Mom: *"We miss you, Renee. It's not the same without you. Please come."*

Her throat tightened. She could practically hear her mother's voice in the message—soft, loving, endlessly patient. But what would she even say if she called back?

"Sorry, Mom, I can't. I have work."

It was always her excuse. It had been her armor for years. And yet, standing in the silence of her immaculate condo with a half-empty takeout box on the table, it felt paper-thin. Renee sat back down at the table and reached for her fork again, shoveling food she didn't want into her mouth just to keep herself from crying. She wouldn't cry. Not tonight. "Work pays the bills," she muttered to herself, like a mantra. "Work pays the bills."

But as the night stretched on, and the snow fell heavier outside her window, Renee felt the truth gnawing at her in the quiet. Work might pay the bills, but it couldn't buy her companionship. It couldn't replace the sound of her mother's laugh, the teasing voices of her siblings, or the warmth of a family cabin filled with love and noise. And it couldn't fill the hollow space in her chest that grew wider every time she let a call ring unanswered. The condo was equipped with everything she could possibly want or need. The condo was her fortress.

And Renee had never felt so alone.

An Uninvited Guest

The next morning, Renee arrived early at work and sat in her corner office, planning to close out deals before Christmas Eve. She sipped black coffee as she scanned her emails—until one stood out.

Subject Line: *"Are you fulfilled, Renee?"*

Confused, Renee clicked it. The message was short: *"You're successful, Renee Carrington. But if you scrooge, you lose. You'll see soon enough. A Friend."* Her heart jolted. Was this a prank? Before she could think further, the lights flickered. Her desk phone rang—only static on the other end. *Was this the universe's cruel joke?*

Later into the early start of that same evening, Renee's office was silent except for the soft ticking of the wall clock. She leaned back in her chair, scanning her unread emails as the day's light faded. It would soon be Christmas, but Renee didn't care. Her mind was locked on work, and any distractions; family, friends, or herself—could wait. Then came a knock. She froze, staring at the glass office door. *Who comes here this late?*

"Come in," she called, expecting security or maintenance.

Instead, the door opened, and there he was—David Bennett. Renee's breath caught as she blinked in disbelief. He looked the same: tall, dark, handsome, rugged in that warm, approachable way. The man she once knew, with his easy smile and steady presence, but his eyes now held something sharper—like they'd seen a version of her he didn't recognize.

"David?" Her voice cracked, betraying her.

"Evening, Renee," he said, stepping inside. He glanced around the sterile office, taking in her achievements, awards on walls, shelves, a perfectly organized desk. "Nice to see you haven't changed. Busy as ever, I see."

Her chest tightened. "What…what are you doing here?" David shrugged, but there was weight behind the casual gesture.

"I'm back in town visiting family for Christmas. I thought I'd drop by. I wasn't sure if you'd still be here, but then again…" He looked pointedly at her laptop, still glowing.

"You've been waiting five years to make that dig?", she shot back, trying to sound unaffected.

He chuckled softly, his gaze steady. "Not at all. Just curious, I guess."

The words hung heavy in the air. Renee stood, smoothing her blazer, trying to regain her composure. *David Bennett.* The man who proposed to her. Five years ago, he'd knelt in her old apartment, a modest but beautiful ring in his hands and love in his eyes, asking her to build a life with him. He'd wanted a family, a future together. But Renee wanted…more. *"You're a great man, David,"* she'd told him then. *"But I can't give you what you want. I just got offered the VP promotion today. I can't slow down. Not now."*

It had been a clean break, or so she'd thought. She traded the dream of marriage and children for a corner office and a paycheck that others envied. And yet, seeing him now, a knot she refused to acknowledge tightened in the pit of her stomach.

"You didn't have to come here," she said quietly, folding her arms. "If you came here to make me feel guilty about my choices, don't bother. I don't regret anything."

He raised a brow, unconvinced. "Don't you?"

Renee swallowed and took a deep breath. "No. I built the life I wanted." David tilted his head, that unreadable gaze cutting right through her.
"You built a life, Renee. But do you *live* it?"

The words landed harder than she cared to admit. She turned away, pretending to gaze out her window watching the sun setting outside.
"Is this why you came? To play armchair therapist?"
"No," David said softly. "I came because I saw your mom earlier today when she was getting staples for the cabin. She mentioned you'd probably be here alone tonight, like every night. I thought…" He paused, choosing his words.
"I thought maybe you'd want to see a familiar face."

Renee clenched her jaw, fighting the sudden sting behind her eyes. She hated this—his kindness, his ability to see through her walls.
"You didn't have to," she whispered.
"I know." David looked at her, long and steady, before adding quietly, "But I wanted to."

She finally turned to face him, feeling stripped bare in a way that unnerved her. For years, Renee had convinced herself she'd made the right call. She told herself love and family were nice ideas for other people—people who weren't trying to survive in a cutthroat world. But now, standing in front of the man who'd once loved her—who'd *chosen* her—she felt it. That small, splintered regret she'd buried so deep, she almost believed it wasn't there.

"Renee," David said softly, pulling her from her thoughts. "I hope you're happy. I really do."

Something cracked inside her, just for a moment, and she looked at him, her voice softer than she meant it to be.

"Are *you* happy?"

David smiled faintly. "I am. It's not the life I imagined with *you,* but it's good."

The honesty in his voice burned. He stepped toward the door, pausing just as his hand hit the knob. "Take care of yourself, Renee. Merry Christmas." The door closed behind him with a finality that made the room feel colder.

Renee sank into her chair, staring at the space where he'd stood. *Do you live it?* She'd thought of the reports on her desk, the silent empty condo waiting for her, and the unopened text from her mother inviting her to the cabin. Renee Carrington had everything she wanted, didn't she? The steady click of her banging the keys of her laptop seemed deafening now, a reminder of her hollow fortress. For the first time in years, Renee let herself sit with it—the ache of what might have been. And it hurt, bad.

3

Lessons From a Familiar Face

That night, Renee fell into an uneasy sleep on her couch. When she woke up, the room wasn't her high-rise condo anymore—it was her childhood cabin her family owned in Asheville. The smell of cinnamon and pine filled the air, and she could hear the sound of children laughing and adults singing along to Christmas carols. Renee stood in the cabin's quiet living room, frowning at the fireplace.

Snow fell thick and steady outside the window and her family's laughter echoed faintly from the kitchen, but she felt strangely disconnected from it all. Her mother had insisted she take charge of the fire… *"Something to keep you busy, so you're not checking your email,"* and Renee begrudgingly agreed. She crouched low, poking the smoldering logs, coaxing flames back to life. "Come on," she muttered. She leaned further in, trying to move the stubborn wood. And then—*CRACK.* The back of her head collided hard with the edge of the heavy wooden mantle as she stood up too quickly. "Ugh!" Renee winced and stumbled backward, pressing a hand to her scalp as stars danced before her eyes. The room tilted and wavered like heat rising from summer pavement.

"Renee?"

The voice startled her. Her eyes fluttered open—the world around her definitely wasn't the same. The furniture was different: the floral couch from her childhood, old lace curtains swaying gently. The fire roared, larger and much brighter than before.

"Daddy?"

There he was—her father, standing in the doorway, wearing the red-and-green Christmas sweater she hadn't seen in fifteen years, the one he hadn't worn since he passed away when Renee was 20. He smiled warmly, his presence as solid and real as the cabin around them.

"Hey, sweetheart," he said softly. Renee blinked, gripping the edge of the hearth.

"No…no, this isn't happening."

He tilted his head with that familiar patience. "Oh, it's happening, Renee. Sit down."

"I hit my head," she whispered, more to herself than to him.

He chuckled. "Maybe you did. Doesn't mean you don't need to hear what I've got to say."

Still disoriented, Renee sank into the old armchair that hadn't existed moments ago. She stared at her father, afraid to blink in case he vanished.

"You've been working so hard, Renee," he said. "Always on a mission. Always running. But running toward *what?*"

"I've been building something," she argued weakly. "A life. Success, daddy."

"Success?" Her father's brow furrowed, his tone kind but pointed. "You think this is what success looks like? Alone? Having a fancy corner office? Cold empty condo? Alone at Christmas?"

"I'm *not* alone." she replied.

Her father raised an eyebrow. "Aren't you?" The words stung because they were true. Renee stood and wrapped her arms around herself, staring at the flames.

"I'm doing what I'm supposed to do. Working hard. Winning."

Her father shook his head gently. "Winning what, Renee? This isn't a game you can win alone."

Tears pricked her eyes, uninvited and unexpected. "I don't know how to do anything else, Daddy. If I stop, I lose everything I've worked for." Her father moved closer, crouching in front of her, his face lined with a mix of love and sadness.

"You're losing more than you realize right now. Family. Connection. Yourself." He rested a warm hand on her shoulder. "No human is an island, sweetheart. Not even you."

She mumbled. "This can't be real."

"Renee?"

"Yes, Daddy?" Her voice cracked. He smiled warmly. "You've been busy, have you? So busy you forgot this feeling?" He asked, pointing around the cabin.

"I don't have time for—"

"Family? Love? Laughter?" he finished for her. "You're alone, Renee, and not because you *have* to be. Because you *chose* to be."

Tears pricked her eyes as the sounds of her mother and siblings rang louder. Her dad's voice softened. "Remember these words I say to you: 'If you scrooge, you lose'."

And just like that he wasn't there.

4

Choices

Renee jolted awake on her couch, her heart pounding. The words echoed in her mind: *"If you scrooge, you lose."* She glanced at her phone. A voicemail blinked from her mother: *"Renee, we're at the cabin. I hope you'll come. Even if it's just for one day."* Renee's chest tightened. She thought of the last time she'd been around her family—five years ago—and how their smiles and banter had felt foreign to her. How she'd rolled her eyes while they danced in the kitchen. *"You're alone because you chose to be."* Her father's words rang in her ears. It was the first time she realized her life—her so-called success—was a fortress. And she was the only prisoner inside.

Renee sat slumped on the edge of the couch, starring. Her hand instinctively drifted to the tender bump on the back of her head—a reminder of the strange, vivid encounter she wasn't ready to explain to herself. Her mother's voicemail still echoed in her mind: *"We're at the cabin. I hope you'll come. Even if it's just*

for one day." Renee's chest tightened again. *One day.*
Could she give them that much?

She thought of the last time she'd been around
her family, a Christmas gathering five years ago. The
cabin had been the same—warm, rustic, smelling of pine
and cinnamon, but everything about *her* had felt out of
place. She'd shown up late, fresh from a conference call
and wearing an immaculate off-white wool coat that
didn't quite belong amongst her cousins' hoodies, wacky
Christmas socks, jeans and ugly Christmas sweaters. Her
laptop had stayed tucked under her arm like a shield, and
she ignored the disapproving glances from her siblings as
she checked emails over the turkey dinner.

Renee could still see the memory play out in her
mind: her brother Malcolm cranking up The
Temptations' version of '*Silent Night*' on an old
bluetooth speaker while her mother rolled her eyes and
rocked fondly to that old school version.

"Alright, let's do this," Malcolm had grinned, pulling
their cousins, nieces and nephews into a messy Soul Train
line around the cabin. Everyone danced. Everyone
laughed. Her mother swayed and hummed along as
cousins twirled each other across the carpet. Even her
reserved younger sister, Jackie, broke out into an

exaggerated two-step that had everyone in stitches. Renee had watched it all from the couch, perched like a visitor who didn't belong.

"Come on, Renee!" Jackie had shouted, reaching for her hand. Renee had pulled back, shaking her head with a smile that didn't reach her eyes.

"I'm good. You guys have fun." And they had. Their voices and laughter filled the space as they danced into the kitchen to raid the fridge for leftovers. Renee, meanwhile, had grabbed her laptop, clinging to the one thing that made her feel valuable.

Later, when the group moved to caroling—her mom leading the charge with her smooth alto voice—Renee quietly slipped out onto the porch, using "work" as her excuse. She remembered standing there alone, cold breath fogging up the air, the music muffled behind the cabin walls. She'd watched the lights from inside flicker through the frost-kissed windows. Smiles. Banter. Togetherness. And there she was, *lonely* in a room full of people who loved her and now standing outside freezing on the front porch.

She could see it so clearly now—how her pride had built a wall between herself and all of them. How she'd chosen isolation even as they reached for her.

That Christmas had ended with awkward hugs and her mother's soft voice asking, "You sure you're okay, baby?"

"I'm fine, Mom," Renee had said. But she hadn't been. And now she was sitting in the stillness of her empty condo with the weight of her choices pressed down on her chest. Her father's words echoed faintly in her mind: *"No man is an island, sweetheart. Not even you."*

For five years, Renee had convinced herself that she was better off alone—that her sacrifices had been worth the price. But what if they hadn't? What if all this time, she'd been running so hard toward *success* that she'd left love, laughter, and life behind? The phone buzzed in her hand again. Another text from her mom: *"We're playing the Lose Your Black Card game tonight, and Malcolm's trash-talking everyone like always. Wish you were here, baby."* Renee stared at the screen for a long moment. Then, without overthinking, she grabbed her boots and coat. The condo was spotless. Her career was thriving. But Renee realized she was done choosing loneliness.

Maybe there was still time to change.

Finding Her Way Back

The drive to the cabin felt longer than Renee remembered. Snow flurries danced across the windshield of her Range Rover and the road was quiet except for the soft hum of her all-wheel-drive engine. As she got closer, her heartbeat quickened, and a creeping doubt settled in her mind. *What if they're mad I stayed away so long? What if it's awkward?*

She pulled up to the familiar cabin, its pitched roof dusted in snow, golden light spilling warmly from the windows. From inside, she could hear faint music and bursts of laughter. Her family—*her* people—were all there. Renee sat in the car for a moment, her fingers gripped tightly around the steering wheel. She glanced at the gas station tin of cookies in the passenger seat and shook her head. *What am I even doing here?* But before she could talk herself into backing the car out of the driveway, the front door swung open. Her mother stepped onto the wraparound porch, bundled in a thick cardigan, her face breaking into a wide, disbelieving smile. "Renee? Is that you?" Renee froze, then smiled sheepishly through the windshield. Her mom waved her arms excitedly like a woman half her age.

"Get in here, girl! It's freezing!" As Renee climbed out of the car, the cold hit her face, but her mother's hug was warm, solid, and *real*.

"You came," her mom whispered, squeezing her tight.

"Yeah, Mom. I did." Her mom pulled back, searching Renee's face with tear-brimmed eyes.

"You're just in time. Everyone's inside—and I hope you're hungry." Renee stood outside the snow-covered Asheville cabin, clutching the tin of cookies she'd picked up at a gas station on the way.

"Get in here, child! It's freezing!" Her mom called out to her once again.

The noise hit her first as she stepped into the cabin. Laughter, music, chatter. Kids shrieked as they ran through the hallway, someone called out a challenge over the card game, and the smell of something savory and nostalgic wafted through the air. Her belly growled with hunger.

"Look who's here!" her mom announced loudly. Heads turned, and for a beat, the room fell silent—then erupted into joy.

"Renee!" Everyone happily yelled. Her brother Malcolm was the first to stride over, grinning from ear to ear.

"Wow, the workaholic showed up!"

"Boy, don't start," Renee shot back with a smirk, pointing her finger at him. Her sister Jackie appeared next, pulling her into a hug.

"We missed you, sis. Don't you dare ghost us again."

"I missed you, too," Renee said softly, surprising herself with how much she meant it. Within moments, she was surrounded—cousins clapping her on the back, nieces tugging at her coat sleeves, asking if she brought gifts (she hadn't, of course), and her mom proudly escorting her into the kitchen as if Renee were a celebrity making an appearance.

"Sit, sit!" her mom insisted, shoving a plate in front of her piled high with turkey, mac and cheese, and greens. She placed a slice of sweet potato pie in front of Renee, with a tall cold glass of sweet tea.

Renee found herself at the long, wooden dining table—so familiar, yet foreign—with her family bantering and teasing across from her. Malcolm was bragging about his card game wins while Jackie rolled her eyes. The kids bickered loudly about who ate the last of the tin cookies she brought. The warmth of it all, the noise, the chaos—*it felt like home.* The laptop and emails that had anchored her every thought for years now seemed so distant, so insignificant. *"Work pays the bills,"* she had always told herself. But right now, surrounded by these people who loved her in ways no job could, that phrase didn't cross her mind. Not once.

After dinner, someone, probably Malcolm, cranked up the old bluetooth speaker with Donny Hathaway's *This 'Christmas'*.

"Alright, y'all know what time it is," he grinned.

"Oh, no. Not this again," Renee teased.

"Girl, don't act brand new," Jackie shot back, grabbing her hand and dragging her up from her seat. Before Renee could protest, she was in the living room, Malcolm leading a line of kids and cousins into a chaotic Soul Train line. Jackie spun her in a circle, laughing like they were kids again, and this time, Renee didn't pull back. She joined in. She danced. She twirled nieces until they were dizzy and giggling. She sang along, off-key and shameless, to carols she hadn't sung in years. Malcolm caught her eye at one point and gave her an exaggerated two thumbs-up, shouting, "Now that's the Renee I remember!" For the first time in longer than she could remember, Renee laughed until her stomach hurt. She felt the tension in her shoulders melt away, the walls she had built so carefully around herself cracking open.

Later that night, as she curled up on the couch with her mom and Jackie—listening to her brother loudly lose at cards in the next room—Renee felt it deep in her bones: *she belonged here.* This messy, imperfect, loud group of people was her anchor. She'd spent five years running from them, convincing herself that her worth was measured in promotions and paychecks. But nothing could compare to this—to being wrapped in love, to feeling like herself again. Her mother squeezed her hand gently. "See, baby? We've been waiting for you to come home." Renee blinked back the sudden burn in her eyes. "I know, Mom. I'm sorry it took me so long." Her mother smiled warmly. "Well, you're here now. That's all that matters." And not once, had Renee thought about her emails, her spreadsheets, or the calls she might have missed. She didn't think about proving herself or working harder. She just *was.* And it felt like winning in the truest sense of the word.

5

The Rebuild

Later that night, as her family sat around the fire, her mother asked, "How's work, sweetheart?" Renee hesitated, then shrugged.

"It's… fine."

"What about life?" her mom added. The fire crackled softly as the Carrington family settled into their favorite spots around the cabin's cozy living room. Blankets were draped over everyone's laps, mugs of hot chocolate steamed in hands, and the quiet lull of contentment filled the space. The chaos of dinner and dancing had given way to a calm, intimate warmth.

Renee moved to the hearth, her back to the fire's glow, her knees pulled close as she watched her family. Her mother sat in her favorite armchair, knitting absentmindedly, while Jackie lightly dozed under a blanket nearby. Malcolm was still at the dining table, pretending to explain the rules of spades to a group of kids. Renee looked around at her family cuddling their kids, her cousins whispering to their spouses, and her mother watching her. She swallowed hard and moved to a recliner.

"I think…I think I've been working too hard for the wrong things," she said quietly. Her mother smiled knowingly. "You don't have to win alone, Renee." Tears threatened again, but this time she didn't push them back. She let herself feel *all of it*—the regret, the relief, the joy. And for the first time in years, Renee felt peaceful. No buzzing phone, no glaring emails, no imaginary clock ticking over her shoulder. Just this. The fire. The people. The love. But something in her still stirred—a knot in her chest she knew she couldn't leave unspoken. Her mother's voice broke the silence.

"You look like you've got something on your mind, sweetheart." Renee looked up, startled to find her mother's eyes gently watching her. Jackie stirred awake, and even Malcolm wandered over, drawn by the shift in the room's energy. One by one, her family turned their attention to her. Renee swallowed hard, the words gathering like a lump in her throat.

"I…" She paused, her voice barely above a whisper. "I need to say something." Her family waited quietly, expectantly, their eyes soft and understanding. Renee exhaled shakily.

"I'm sorry." Her mother tilted her head.

"Sorry for what, baby?"

"For… all of it," Renee said, her voice stronger now.
"For being so caught up in work that I missed everything.
I missed *you*—your birthdays, your phone calls, dinners,
holidays. I've spent years convincing myself that work
was all that mattered, that I needed to prove something to
the world. But…I don't even know who I was trying to
prove it to." Her words hung in the air, heavy and raw.

"I told myself I was winning," Renee continued, her gaze
moving between them, "but I was lonely. I *am* lonely."
Her voice cracked, and she bit her lip, fighting tears.
"And it's my fault. I worked so hard to climb some ladder
that I built a life where there was no room for anyone
else. Not for David, not for friends, not for you."

Her mother set her knitting down, her face soft
with love. Malcolm moved closer to sit on the arm of her
chair, leaning in. Jackie shifted to sit up straighter, her
eyes brimming with compassion. Renee shook her head,
tears slipping freely now.

"I've been scared to admit it—that I made the wrong
choices. That I worked so hard I missed out on the things
that matter most. And the worst part is, you all *tried* to

reach me. You invited me. You loved me anyway. I just…
I didn't show up." Silence settled briefly, punctuated by
the gentle snap and pop of the fire. Her mother stood and
crossed the room, leaning in to pull Renee into her arms.
"Baby, we love you. We always have. And we always
will."

Renee let herself cry then, her shoulders shaking as
her mother held her tightly. She held her mom back.
Malcolm broke the silence with his signature humor.
"About time, sis. I thought you'd *never* admit we're the
best part of your life." Laughter rippled through the room.
Jackie grinned, reaching over to pat Renee's knee.
"It's not too late, you know. We're not going anywhere."

Renee looked at each of them—her mother's soft,
unwavering gaze, Malcolm's teasing grin, Jackie's
understanding smile. Her chest felt lighter, like a weight
she didn't even realize she'd been carrying had finally
lifted.

"I want to do better," Renee said softly. "I want to show up
for real this time. Not just for Christmas, but for
everything." Her mother cupped Renee's face, smiling
warmly.

"Then do it, baby. You don't have to prove anything to us.
Just be here," she added, wiping at her daughter's tears

with her thumb. Renee nodded, wiping her face and laughing at herself as Malcolm tossed the tissue box to her.

"Does this mean you're coming to our annual karaoke disaster tomorrow?" Jackie teased. Renee groaned, shaking her head.

"Uggh, you guys still do that?" Her mother laughed, the sound filling the room like sunlight.

"Oh, you're singing, Renee. No way around it." Malcolm clapped his hands together.

"I'm picking your song. You're welcome."

The teasing and laughter flowed easily, and Renee sat back, soaking it all in. For the first time in as long as she could remember, she didn't feel like an outsider watching from a distance. She was *part of it.* The rebuilding of her relationships, her connection to her family—it was happening right here, in the messy, loving chaos of this cabin. Her family had never stopped waiting for her, and now, she was finally choosing them.

As the fire crackled and voices rose again in banter and jokes, Renee smiled through her tears. Work might pay the bills, but *this*—this love, this laughter, this life— was what made her whole…

…That night, five years ago, the ring went into a drawer. That chapter closed. But now, five years later, she'd opened it again…

<u>Present Day-New Year's Eve</u>

The click of her heels echoed hollow through her entryway as Renee stepped inside her apartment, the door shutting behind her with a soft finality. The distant hum of city life still murmured through the window, but inside it was just her and the silence. She didn't bother turning on the lights. The moonlight filtered in, soft and silver, brushing across the hardwood floor and the framed photographs she hadn't moved in years. The party had ended hours ago; another successful charity gala for the books, but her mind wasn't on the donors or the thank-you speeches. It was on *him*. David.

The ballroom shimmered beneath cascading crystal chandeliers, each flickering light like a heartbeat echoing in Renee's chest. The annual New Year's Eve charity gala was in full swing—waiters weaving through the crowd with champagne flutes, a jazz quartet breathing life into the golden air, and the scent of peonies and politics floating in the air. Renee stood poised in her form fitted black velvet strapless gown, sipping slowly, her laughter effortless, her smile immaculate…until *he* walked in. He wasn't supposed to be here. Or maybe he was—he was always well connected, always invited. But seeing him after their last encounter still made the room spin like it used to.

He looked devastatingly good. Clad in a tailored midnight blue tuxedo that hugged his broad frame perfectly, his presence pulled attention without asking for it. The years had only refined him—salt at his temples, a stronger jawline, and that calm, commanding energy that made him seem untouchable. His tie was simple, but his eyes…those eyes still held every answer to questions she'd once been too afraid to ask.

They didn't speak. Not that night. There were too many eyes, too many whispers, too many walls. But across the crowd, his gaze found hers. Brief. Quiet. Undeniable. And just like that, she was taken back. She had watched him from across the ballroom tonight. Watched the way he smiled at people, warm and effortless. The way he still tugged at the cuffs of his sleeves when he was nervous, a habit she knew like her own heartbeat. He had looked good—too good. And too far away, even when he stood just a few feet from her.

She exhaled slowly, the memory of *that night* playing in her mind like an old film reel on repeat. The garden lights. The champagne. The ring box she never opened again. She had been too caught up in her career, too blinded by ambition to see what he was really offering. And when he asked her anyway—when he knelt before her after everyone had gone—he hadn't just asked for her hand…he had offered his whole heart. And she didn't say no. Actually, she didn't say anything because at the time, *saying nothing* felt safer than telling him the truth; that she was afraid. That she didn't know how to be the woman who chased her dreams *and* came home to someone. That she was afraid she'd let him down. That he'd leave eventually when he realized she'd never be the soft, stay-at-home version of love that so many men wanted. But David never wanted her to shrink. He just wanted her to *choose him, too.*

She crossed into her bedroom. Her three-inch heels dug softly into her plush elegant winter white carpet as she unzipped the velvet gown with careful fingers, letting it slip from her body like the mask she'd worn all night. He was back in town—or still in town? Successful. Sexy. Handsome. Everything he'd always been, and then some. The world had opened for him, and he had risen to meet it, just like she knew he would. But none of it dulled the quiet ache that had taken up permanent residence in her chest.

She moved toward the bureau, her breath shaky. Opened the top drawer. It creaked open like it hadn't been touched in years. And there it was. The small box. The one she couldn't bear to throw away. It was still wrapped in the navy satin ribbon he'd used the night he proposed, slightly frayed at the edges now, softened by time. She reached for it with reverent fingers, then sat on the edge of the bed in her bra and panties and pulled it close, pressing it to her chest like it still held the pulse of that moment. The tears came slowly. Quietly. A warm trail down her cheeks as she closed her eyes and remembered every word he said that night five years ago.
"You don't have to be ready for forever right now. Just say yes to building it together." And still…she hadn't.

She didn't need to open it. She remembered—how her breath had caught, how her heart had stuttered, how her silence had ended everything. "I should've said yes," she whispered to the quiet room. "I should've said yes a long time ago," she whispered into the darkness. A box never reopened. A ring never worn. A love never lived.

She hugged it tighter, as if that might turn back time. But the truth was inescapable—David was back. And she was still in love with the one she let get away. But it wasn't too late. Not yet.

That same night, David loosened his tie as he stepped into the quiet of his penthouse suite. The gala had been a blur of polite smiles, handshakes, and conversations that skimmed the surface. But through all the small talk and sophistication, his mind had been locked on one thing. One *woman*. Renee. He hadn't expected to see her tonight. Hadn't prepared for the jolt her presence would deliver—the same way she always used to disarm him without saying a word. She hadn't changed since the night he visited her office before Christmas. Still elegant. Still composed. Still sophisticated. But her eyes…they gave her away. He saw the flicker of something when their gazes met. Recognition. Memory. *Longing.*

David poured himself a glass of Louis XIII Cognac and stepped out onto the balcony to clear his head. The city lights stretched wide beneath him, a patchwork of everything he'd built since she turned him down. He was successful, sure. Respected. Secure. But none of it filled the space where she once lived in him. He had loved her with everything he had. Still did, if he was honest. She had been the plan, the future. The *yes* he wanted more than any deal or promotion. And she hadn't given it.

David let out a breath, his hands tightening around the glass. He hadn't been angry that she said no. Just…broken. And even now, five years later, seeing her again…twice, had reopened a door he thought he'd finally sealed shut. Was she thinking about it too? Was she remembering the night he proposed in her living room, how he lost his voice even though he rehearsed it a thousand times? He leaned against the railing, the cool air brushing against his skin. Maybe it wasn't over. Maybe it never really had been.

6

Second Chances

Renee sat at her desk a week later, her office window reflecting the warm glow of the New Year. The holidays had shaken something loose in her, and for once, she welcomed it. A notification popped up: *"Urgent work happy hour tonight at 6:00!."* She smiled and clicked the decline option. Instead, Renee picked up her phone to call her mom.

"Hey mom, I'm thinking of hosting Sunday dinner at my place. Catered of course. You know I can't cook nearly as good as you and Jackie." Her mother's surprised laughter echoed on the line. In the end, Renee learned the truth: *If you scrooge, you lose.* And winning, it turned out, had nothing to do with the boardroom. It was about showing up—for family, for love, and for herself.

February had rolled in quietly. Renee sat working at her desk in her corner office, but for the first time, the view of the sprawling city skyline didn't feel like success. It just felt…quiet. The usual satisfaction she used to get from a clear inbox or a completed report was gone. Instead, she felt something else—hopeful, uncertain, but alive.

Her holiday spent with her family had changed something deep within her. She was still Renee Elise Carrington—ambitious, driven, a woman who got things done—but the walls she'd built around herself were starting to crack. And for once, she wasn't afraid. A soft knock interrupted her thoughts.

"Come in," she called, expecting her assistant, Lila. The door opened, and there he was again—David Bennett.

Renee froze. She blinked twice, wondering if she was just imagining him like that strange occurrence when she bumped her head and saw her dad in a surreal dream. But no—this was real. He stood in the doorway holding a flat-wrapped gift in his hands, wearing a navy L.L. Bean sweater, jeans and a tan shearling coat that made him look effortlessly warm and impeccably handsome.

"David?" Her voice cracked.

"Hey, Renee." His voice was calm, soft, as though he wasn't intruding on her carefully orchestrated world.

"Hope I'm not interrupting."

"No—no, not at all." She stood, smoothing her blazer nervously. "What are you…doing here?" He took a step forward, his familiar gaze settling on hers.

"A little birdy told me that it was your birthday yesterday. I figured I'd stop by to say happy birthday in person." Her heart clenched.

"You didn't have to—"

"I wanted to," he interjected. He placed the gift on her desk. It was neatly wrapped in silver paper with a simple ribbon, nothing flashy or over the top—just like David. Renee stared at it, overwhelmed by the quiet gesture.

"You remembered my birthday?" she asked, her voice softer now.

"Always," he replied, his eyes holding hers for a long moment. Renee swallowed hard, sitting back down and pulling the gift closer to her.

"Thank you," she said, almost shyly. "You really didn't have to do this."

"I wanted to," he repeated gently.

She untied the ribbon and unwrapped the box, her hands trembling slightly. Inside was a spiral, hardcover notebook. She recognized it instantly—it was just like the one she used to carry years ago when they first started dating, where she'd scribble plans, dreams, and to-do lists. Opening the first page, she found his handwriting:

"To starting over, or picking up where we left off. Your choice, if you'll allow me. - David"

Her breath hitched, and she looked up, her eyes searching his. "David…" she whispered. Renee stood up. He smiled faintly, slipping his hands into his pockets. "I've been thinking about you, Renee. I never really stopped. When I saw you at Christmas, then again at the gala, I realized that I couldn't walk away again without saying this: I still love you. I don't know if that's what you want to hear, or if it's too much, but…it's the truth. No one else could ever replace you."

Her heart pounded as she struggled to process his words. *He still loves me? After everything?* David stepped closer, his voice steady.

"I know things didn't work out between us before. You were focused on your dreams, and I get that. But it doesn't mean we can't try again." He hesitated, then added, "We don't have to pick up exactly where we left off. We can start over, take things slow. I just want another chance, Renee."

She stared at him, her mind reeling. Five years ago, she'd chosen work over love, telling herself she couldn't have both. But standing here now, looking at

David—this man who still believed in her, who still *loved* her—she realized something she hadn't let herself admit until now: she'd been wrong.

"I don't know what to say," Renee whispered, her voice shaky. "I…I didn't think you'd still feel this way." David smiled softly.

"I've always felt this way." Tears pricked at her eyes as the weight of his words settled over her.

"I've changed, David. At least, I'm trying to. I don't want to be that person who puts work before everything else anymore."

"Good," he said gently. "Because I want the version of you that *shows up.* Not just for work, but for life."

A long silence stretched between them, filled with unspoken words and old memories. Finally, Renee smiled through her tears, her voice steady this time.

"Okay." David raised an eyebrow.

"Okay?"

"Let's start over," she said, a small laugh escaping her lips. "You're right. It doesn't have to be what it was before. But I want to try." He grinned, that warm, familiar smile that made her chest flutter.

"I'll take it." He stepped closer, brushing a strand of hair away from her face.

"Happy birthday, Renee." He kissed her on the cheek, then gently embraced her.

For the first time in years, Renee felt like she was stepping toward something real—toward love, laughter, and connection. For so long, she'd believed her worth was tied to her work, but now, in her corner office with David Bennett standing in front of her, holding her, she knew that she didn't have to choose between success and happiness. Maybe she really *could* have both.

"Thank you, David," she whispered. He grinned again. "How about dinner soon? Nothing fancy. Just us catching up." Renee smiled back, nodding.

"I'd like that."

As David turned to leave, Renee looked down at the notebook in her hands, the words on the first page still pulling at her heart: *To starting over, or picking up where we left off, if you'll allow me. Your choice.* For once, the choice was easy. And this time, she wasn't letting love slip away.

Let's Stay Together

Renee Carrington stared at the text on her phone, her heart having a strange mix of trepidation and hope. It was from David Bennett. Prior to Christmas, they hadn't spoken in well over five years—not since their what was supposed to be a perfect engagement unraveled in a storm of unmet expectations, misunderstandings, and words unspoken. Yet here he was. He had moved back to the city. She saw him at the New Year's Eve gala. Then he showed up the day after her birthday and kept his promise to try to make it work, no matter what, asking now if they could meet for coffee. Just coffee. She hesitated before responding but ultimately typed, *"Okay. Let me know when and where."*

David was already at the café when Renee arrived. The familiar sight of him made her stomach flip. He stood as she approached, his warm brown eyes soft with apology.

"Renee," he said, his voice just as she remembered. He touched her elbows and leaned in to give her a soft kiss on the cheek.

"David." She nodded, her voice steady, though her emotions were anything but. They exchanged pleasantries before David cut to the heart of the matter.

"Look, I've spent the past month thinking about everything I did wrong. Everything *we* did wrong. And I know I asked to start over. Even if it's just as friends." Renee studied him, surprised by the humility in his tone. There had been moments during their breakup when both of their pride had built a wall between them. But now, he seemed different—softer, more grounded.

"I don't know what starting over looks like," she admitted, "but I think we can try."

It began slowly. A week after she met David for coffee, Renee received a bouquet of deep burgundy calla lilies at her office. No card. No name. But she knew. He used to bring them to her after difficult work weeks—the kind of gesture that said, *'I see you, even when you don't say a word.'* She stared at the flowers for a long time before placing them on her desk.

Two days later, she ran into him. It wasn't an accident. She stepped into her favorite café on 9th and

Laurel—the same place she'd nursed countless Sunday lattes and drafted dreams in a leather-bound journal—and there he was, already seated at the corner table, the one near the window. David looked up and smiled, that same quiet smile that had once unraveled her with a glance. "Didn't expect to see you here," he said. But they both knew he had.

"Still love the espresso here," she offered, pretending her pulse hadn't just tripled. They didn't sit together that day, but he rose when she left, gently touching her arm.

"Renee," he said softly. "I'm glad to see you again." Something in her chest fluttered, but she said nothing. Just nodded and walked away, her heart thudding all the way home.

Then came the emails. Short. Polite. Always with intention.

Subject: That café

Body: The cappuccino art is still terrible. But the coffee's better now. -D

Two days later, she replied.

Subject: Still dramatic, I see

Body: It was a latte. And the leaf design was *almost*

perfect. Don't start. Lol. -R

It continued like that—warmth, laughter, the reawakening of a rhythm they hadn't shared in years. He didn't rush. Didn't pry. He simply *showed up*. At gallery openings he knew she'd attend. At the lecture she gave at the university on marketing strategies. A latte left for her on her office assistant Lila's desk, just the way she liked it, with a sticky note: *"In case today's one of those days."* Then one Sunday, he invited her to brunch.

"No pressure," he said. "Just food, sunlight, and a table by the window." And she said yes.

There, with the sound of clinking glasses and light jazz strumming in the background, she looked at him fully for the first time since the night she walked away.

"You never stopped loving me, did you?" she whispered. He didn't answer immediately. Just reached across the table, softly brushed his thumb along her knuckles.

"No," he said. "I was patiently waiting for you to love me back." The silence was thick. Sacred.

"I never stopped either," she said, her voice barely there. The wind outside shifted. Something inside her opened.

Over the next few weeks, they met for walks in the park, lunches, and even a late-night call when David needed advice about a work project. When David moved back home, he decided to start an entrepreneurship journey and wanted to be as close to Renee as possible. They agreed to no more late work nights or putting each other on the back burner.

Slowly, the old warmth began to return, accompanied by a newfound maturity. They were more careful with their words, more willing to listen, and more generous with their laughter. More hugs, definitely. David invited Renee to his niece's birthday party, a casual event that turned unexpectedly poignant when Renee watched him tenderly braid the little girl's hair. She saw a side of him she hadn't fully appreciated before—a man capable of deep care and quiet strength.

"I forgot how good you are with kids," she said later.

"And I forgot how much I missed hearing you laugh," he replied, his eyes lingering on her face.

The tone David set the next time was intimate, respectful, and deeply emotional, highlighting the care he's taking as they slowly rebuild. It was a quiet Wednesday evening when David invited her to dinner at his new brownstone. He had downsized his living, traded the stuffy penthouse life for something more family friendly. No caterers. No reservations. Just the two of them and the warmth of old jazz records spinning on a vintage turntable. Renee arrived just after 7:00, a chilled bottle of vintage wine in her hand and nerves dancing under her skin. He greeted her in the doorway with a smile and an embrace that felt like home. His sleeves were rolled up, an apron slung over his neck, the wonderful scent of garlic and herbs wafting from the kitchen.

"I cooked," he said proudly. "Try not to faint." She laughed.

"Let's see if it's edible first." She teased. "You're braver than I am. I'm a disaster in the kitchen."

Dinner was slow and easy. They talked about everything to nothing; the books they were reading, the people they had become, the time that had folded itself between them. After dessert, David cleared the dishes, and she insisted they wash them together, then he joined her on the couch with two of his delicious signature espressos. He had become quite the chef; fearing he'd be a bachelor all his life, he took cooking lessons a couple years ago. For a long moment, neither of them spoke. The record played on. Then, gently, he asked, "Do you remember that night in August? When I asked you to marry me?" Renee looked down at her cup, her breath catching.

"I never forgot," she said quietly. David watched her, his voice low but steady.

"I wasn't upset that you said no. I was heartbroken that you didn't say anything at all." Her eyes shimmered.

"I was terrified. Not of you. Of myself. Of the possibility that I wasn't enough. That I'd somehow ruin it." He reached for her hand.

"You were always enough. You still are." Tears slipped down her cheeks then. Not dramatic. Not desperate. Just honest.

"I kept the ring," she admitted. "I still have the box. In my drawer." He smiled gently.

"I figured you did. I never bought another one. There'll never be another love besides you." The room went still. Electric. She touched his cheek, her thumb brushing the faint stubble there.

"Do you still want forever with me?" He didn't flinch.

"I never stopped wanting it." She leaned in, forehead against his, tears between them like salt and memory.

"I'm not running this time," she whispered. David held her face in his hands and kissed her like they still had a future to build—because they did.

Two weeks later, the Saturday morning light poured softly into David's kitchen, golden and gentle, as if the universe itself had exhaled peace. He stood at the stove, shirtless, brewing coffee while the scent of cinnamon toast warmed the air. Behind him, barefoot and quiet, Renee leaned against the doorway. She had watched him for a full minute, taking in the curve of his sculpted back, the easy grace of him in his home. *In their new rhythm.* Today felt different. Sacred somehow. She reached into her pocket and gently touched the small velvet box she had kept hidden for so long. It had lived in her drawer like a secret she was never brave enough to tell. But not anymore.

"David?" she called softly. He turned toward her, mug in hand, his expression brightening the way it always did when he looked at her. But then he stopped. She stepped forward, slowly lifting her left hand. The ring—*his ring*—gleamed in the morning light. It was simple and stunning, just like their love. A promise once paused, now renewed without a single word. For a moment, David said nothing. His lips parted, breath caught in his chest. His eyes filled, the kind of tears men don't shed unless something sacred has been returned to them.

"You kept it," he said hoarsely.

"I told you I did," she whispered. "And I'm ready now." He crossed the space between them, his hands cradling hers, thumbs grazing over the ring as if grounding himself in the moment. Then he looked into her eyes.

"This is the most beautiful yes I've ever heard," he murmured. She smiled through tears.

"I figured it was time I finally answered the question." And there, with cinnamon in the air and sunlight painting their new beginning, David pulled her close and kissed her—this time not with longing, but with certainty.

And then one quiet evening under a velvet sky, they had taken a spontaneous weekend trip to the serene coast of the Outer Banks. A windswept cottage, miles of untouched beach, and the kind of stars that whispered of forever. After dinner, David asked her to take a walk with him along the shoreline. The tide was low, the sky dusted with stars, and the moon glowed full above them. Renee didn't suspect anything. Not really. Until she saw it: A small wooden table on the sand, surrounded by lanterns flickering against the breeze. On it: a single glass dome covering a velvet box. *The* box. Her breath caught. David guided her closer, his hand steady on the small of her back. She stared at the box she'd once held in silence— and now saw resting like a promise waiting to be rewritten.

"Same ring," he said softly, lifting the dome and taking the box in his hand. "But this time, I want to ask you again. Not in fear. Not in desperation. But in love, and with hope." He knelt in the sand, just as he had that August night years ago.

"But this time, I'm not asking you to step into forever all at once. I'm asking you to step into *today*. To be my love, my peace, my partner—one day at a time, for as long as you'll have me. Will you marry me, Renee? This time, will you be my forever promise?" He opened the box. The ring still gleamed, but now it held their whole story—the silence, the ache, the slow return, and the rebirth of something real. Renee's hand flew to her mouth. Her eyes spilled over.

"Yes," she whispered, voice trembling. "Yes, David."
He slipped the ring onto her finger, this time with laughter, with light, with a kiss that sealed the years

between them. The stars above them shimmered. The ocean sang below. And in the soft hush of waves and wonder, their forever finally began.

How did he get the ring you ask? He'd been planning it for weeks. Ever since the moment she wore the ring—slipped it onto her finger in the soft glow of morning light and looked at him like she was choosing him, truly choosing him this time. But David wanted to reclaim the moment. Not just receive her yes…but *give her one back.* A new memory. A new beginning.

The problem? She never let that ring out of her sight. She wore it during the day. Slipped it into a velvet pouch at night, tucked beside her journal. And David, ever respectful, never asked for it. So he called in reinforcements: Monique, her oldest friend. The keeper of secrets. The one person Renee trusted to brush her hair during heartbreak and tell her the hard truths without flinching. He invited Monique to brunch under the guise of wanting to "talk about the future." She met him at a discreet café and nearly dropped her mimosa when he explained the plan.

"Wait—you want *me* to get the ring from her?" He nodded, smirking.

"She trusts you. I don't want to snoop. I want it done

right. But I need the ring. I need *that ring* for this." Monique leaned back, arms crossed, clearly intrigued. "You're lucky I believe in second chances."

That night, Monique came over to help Renee prep for their beach weekend; girl-time turned into packing assistant. While Renee was in the shower, Monique gently opened the drawer and slipped the velvet pouch out. Her fingers trembled with nerves, but she smiled to herself. "This is going to be so good," she whispered. She left a small note inside the velvet pouch in its place, folded and tucked it beside the journal, taking the box as well. *Trust the stars. Love always finds its way back.*

The ring was passed to David the next day, delivered in its original box over coffee and a wink. "Don't you dare screw this up," Monique said, handing it over. "I just hope she didn't plan on wearing it today." "I won't," he replied. "Let's hope this plan works." He crossed his fingers. And he didn't screw it up, because on that moonlit beach, with the ring in his possession and love blooming all over again, David gave Renee the proposal she'd never gotten—*the one she deserved.*

Eight months into their engagement, David planned a weekend trip to his lake house they'd regularly visited over the years when they dated. A rustic weekend getaway he had once dreamed of bringing their future family to regularly, to get off the grid once their career goals were in place. At first, Renee was hesitant, painful memories of their broken would-be engagement still haunted her, but she agreed. The weekend was filled with laughter, from cooking mishaps in the compact kitchen to stargazing on the dock to heart-to-heart talks cuddled in front of the firepit. But on the final night, as they sat by the fireplace, David took her hand.

"Renee," he began, his voice trembling slightly, "I've spent the last five years trying to become the man you deserve. And these past eight months, I've felt more alive, more whole, than I ever thought possible. I don't want to waste another moment without you by my side. Let's set a date." Tears welled in Renee's eyes. She had spent so long guarding her heart, but now, she let herself feel the fullness of her love for him. He held her and kissed her like what felt like forever. He never wanted to forget this moment. The engagement was different this time—more grounded, more intentional. It was for real because she said "yes".

They attended pre-marital counseling, set realistic expectations, and worked hard to ensure they were building a partnership based on trust and respect. As they planned their wedding, Renee often marveled at how far they'd come. Their love story wasn't perfect, but it was real—filled with mistakes, forgiveness, and the courage to try again. And when their wedding day finally arrived, surrounded by family and friends, they both knew they were stepping into a future—not as two halves of a whole, but as two complete people choosing each other, every day, for the rest of their lives.

7

The Lavish Wedding, The Talk of the Town

Nestled in the heart of the Blue Ridge Mountains, Asheville provided a breathtaking backdrop for the lavish wedding of this African American couple, who wanted a celebration that reflected their love story, culture, and the beauty of the region, where there were no budgetary restrictions. The couple chose the stunning Cliffs at Walnut Cove, an elite private club offering a sophisticated, opulent setting befitting their rekindled romance and high-profile lifestyles with acres of rolling hills, gardens, and timeless elegance.

The ceremony was set on the lawn of the Club Village, with the stone chapel-inspired clubhouse in the romantic backdrop. A serene space transformed in elegance with fragrant flowers surrounding everyone and everywhere that gave the event a romantic, almost ethereal quality. Guests were greeted by the soft sound of a live harpist playing R&B classics infused with classical tones, setting the perfect ambiance. Rows of gold Chiavari chairs faced an intricately designed floral arch, created from an opulent arrangement of white roses, hydrangeas, and orchids, accented with lush greenery. The Blue Ridge Mountains provided a breathtaking panoramic view, making every guest feel as though they were part of a painting.

The morning of Renee Carrington and David Bennett's wedding dawned crisp and bright, the soft blush of dawn casting a golden glow over the sprawling estate they had chosen as their venue. Set on a lush hillside, the grand estate boasted manicured gardens, and a stunning terrace, and glittered like something out of a fairytale.

Renee sat at the vanity of her bridal suite, robe draped across her shoulders, her makeup untouched and the bustle of bridesmaids humming softly in the next room. In her lap rested the journal David had given her for her birthday. She hadn't journaled in years—that is until David came back. Now its pages were filled again, with stories of *them*. She lifted her pen and paused, her heart tender beneath layers of joy and memory: *Everyone says the beach was our moment. The stars. The ring in that little glass dome. But for me…it wasn't. The moment I came back to him? Really came back? It wasn't a sunset*

proposal or a public reunion. It was that quiet
Wednesday. The night he cooked for me. No audience. No
pressure. Just a cozy dinner for two and jazz and his eyes
across a candlelit table, waiting not for a yes, but for
truth. That's when I realized the man I once ran from was
still the man who made me feel safest in the world. That
night was our real first date. The beginning of us, again.

She pressed the pen down slowly, drawing a single heart in the corner of the page. A small smile curled her lips as she closed the journal and caught her reflection in the mirror. She was ready. Not just to wear the dress. Not just to say, "I do." She was ready to *choose* David again, as he had always chosen her.

Something Borrowed, Something Remembered

The bridal suite filled slowly with laughter, perfume, and the rustle of silk. Renee stood at the center of it all—still, luminous, wrapped in ivory lace and quiet emotion. Renee's gown was a designer masterpiece, a strapless creation of delicate lace and silk that hugged her silhouette before flaring into a dramatic train. The bodice was adorned with subtle beadwork that shimmered like dew drops under the light. Her hair was swept into a loose chignon, with soft tendrils framing her face, and a cathedral veil added a touch of timeless romance.

The bridal suite was abuzz with excitement. Her bridesmaids—her best friends and her sister Jackie, flitted about, helping each other with last-minute touches to their shimmering champagne-colored dresses. Each gown was tailored to complement the individual personality and style of the wearer while creating a cohesive look that screamed elegance. Her best friend and maid of honor, Monique, knelt carefully, adjusting the hem of her gown. "Girl," she whispered, brushing invisible dust from the train, "you are glowing like a chandelier in Versailles."
Renee smiled, eyes glassy.
"Is it too late to change into pajamas and elope?"
Monique grinned.
"Only if I get to wear the pajamas too."

Just then, her mother entered the room, holding a small velvet box—one Renee didn't recognize. Her mother's eyes were already shining.
"I wanted to give you something," she said, voice steady despite the emotion swirling beneath. "From your father."

Renee stood startled. Her mother opened the box, revealing a delicate gold locket on a slender chain. Inside, one side held a tiny black-and-white photo of Renee as a little girl, her father holding her, smiling wide. The other side held a note, written in his neat, familiar script: *"You'll always be my girl. But today, I know you're ready to be someone's forever."*

Renee gasped, the breath catching in her throat. Tears spilled freely now, quiet and full of love. Her mother stepped closer, fastening the necklace around her neck.

"He bought it before he got too sick. Told me to save it for your wedding day." She touched the locket, feeling her father's words beat gently against her heart.

"I miss him," she whispered.

"I know, baby," her mother said softly. "But he's here. You're wearing his love." Monique stepped forward with a tissue, dabbing lightly.

"Okay, no more tears. You've got mascara worth more than my rent on those lashes." The room filled with gentle laughter. Renee turned toward the mirror and saw herself fully—gown, veil, the shimmer of the locket, and the strength in her eyes. She wasn't just a bride. She was a woman carrying love in every form—lost, found, and returned. And she was ready.

The music began—soft strings swelling into a gentle melody that seemed to rise from the floor itself. A string quartet played a moving rendition of "Clair de Lune", their notes floating through the air. The music shifted, cuing the start of the procession. Bridesmaids stepped into view like poetry in motion. Then came her mother, eyes glistening. Then Monique, carrying secrets and sass in equal measure. The guests stood, turning toward the grand double doors as the flower girl gently placed flowers on the runway as she walked to the front of the giant floral pergola. Renee waited behind them, her fingers curled gently around her brother Malcolm's arm. He looked dashing in a tailored black tuxedo, his expression a blend of pride and tenderness. Taking the place of their late father, Malcolm was so honored to be asked to walk her down the aisle. He looked down at her with a warm, steady smile.

"You ready, sis?" She took a breath. Her locket pulsed against her chest, the memory of her father close, as if his spirit had stepped into Malcolm's place for just a moment.

"I am," she whispered.

The doors opened. Gasps echoed softly as Renee stepped into view, the venue bathed in golden light. Every head turned. Every eye found her. But her eyes…they only found David. He stood beneath the floral arch in a tailored black tuxedo, his eyes locked on her like she was the answer to every question he'd ever asked. His chest rose and fell, slow and deep, as if seeing her in that moment made time itself hold its breath, but it was his expression—awed, overwhelmed, utterly in love, that captured everyone's attention.

Renee locked eyes with him the rest of her journey down the aisle, and the world seemed to fall away. His smile captured her. Renee's heels clicked softly against the aisle runner as she and Malcolm slowly moved forward, step by step. Halfway down, she reached for Malcolm's hand, squeezing gently.

"Thank you for walking me." He nodded, blinking hard. "It's an honor, sis", he whispered. When they reached the altar, Malcolm leaned in, kissed her cheek, and whispered, "Go build something beautiful."

David stood at the altar, the murmurs of guests fading into a soft hum behind him. The vows hadn't even begun, but already his heart felt too full for his chest. He adjusted his cuffs on his sleeves for the third time, not because they needed adjusting, but because his hands needed something to do. *She's really going to be my wife today.* The thought came with a quiet ache. Not from fear. From reverence. He had waited for this. Not just through the years apart. Not just since the proposal she couldn't accept. He had waited in the silence after they parted ways, in the ache of unanswered questions, but in the hope he never let die. And somehow, they'd made their way back.

He remembered the moment she wore the ring. No fanfare. No announcement. Just her hand, raised in the morning light, wearing the promise he thought he'd lost forever. And he knew—*she chose me*. On her own terms. In her own time. It made today all the more sacred. Renee stood in ivory and lace, glowing with a softness that made his knees go weak. She handed her beautiful bouquet to Monique. David stepped forward, reaching for her hand. And just like that, she felt it—that grounded warmth that only ever existed when she was beside him.
"Hi," she said softly, unable to stop smiling.
"Hi beautiful," he replied, eyes shining. "You take my breath away."

As they turned to face the officiant, hands intertwined, hearts steady, Renee glanced up at the sky above and quietly thought, *Daddy, I made it. I found my way back to love.* And beneath the gaze of everyone who mattered, she prepared to say the vows she was always meant to speak. As the sun set, the couple exchanged vows in front of 200 loved ones, their heartfelt promises carried on a beautiful mountain view.

The ceremony was officiated by the family pastor, who spoke eloquently about love as a choice, a journey, and a commitment. David's voice was steady as he recited his vows, his words filled with promises to cherish, honor, and respect Renee for the rest of his life. Renee's voice wavered slightly as she spoke, but her words were no less powerful.

"You've taught me that love isn't about perfection, but about perseverance. I promise to choose you, every day, through every joy and every challenge." When the pastor pronounced them husband and wife, David held her face and pulled her into a soft lingering kiss that earned cheers and applause from the guests.

The ceremony also included traditional African American elements in the ceremony, such as the jumping the broom ritual. The broom, hand-decorated with beads and ribbons, was crafted by the bride's mother and sister and symbolized their shared heritage and unity of a love restored. The grand reception tent opened into a candlelit wonderland under the stars, adorned with long banquet tables draped in ivory and gold, each one adorned with rich African prints as runners—bold Ankara and Kente patterns woven between vases of wild orchids, proteas, and lilies. Golden chargers glimmered beneath custom menus embossed with the phrase, *"Where heritage meets happily ever after."*

The space was transformed into a wonderland of elegance and cultural pride. Each place setting featured personalized name cards and hand-tied silk Kente ribbons. Tables were draped in gold and ivory linens, with centerpieces that combined classic floral arrangements with African-inspired accents, such as hand-carved wooden candle holders and textiles in vibrant patterns. Crystal chandeliers hung overhead, their glow creating a magical atmosphere.

While the Bennetts finished their photo session, guests sipped hibiscus tea, passionfruit punch and nibbled on tiny bites while Afrobeat melodies pulsed softly in the background, led by a live band of drummers, harpists, and a talking drum specialist flown in by Renee's mother, because *no daughter of hers* was going to have a wedding without honoring the language of rhythm, surprising their guests with a performance by an African drum and dance troupe that brought vibrant energy to the celebration. The bride and groom's entrance was nothing short of legendary, as the newlyweds entered to thunderous applause, sharing their first dance to *"At Last"* by Etta James. Renee had let her hair down and was ready to get down at her reception. They moved as if no one else existed, their love radiating with every step, their movements intimate and graceful under a canopy of twinkling lights.

After the first dance, Renee and David changed into traditional African wedding attire—she, in a gold and crimson headwrap and a flowing wrap around dress adorned with beadwork; he, in a matching regal agbada with coordinating embroidery. Their hands were joined, arms lifted, and shoulders swaying in perfect rhythm as they danced their way into the reception to Burna Boy's "Destiny," backed by the drums of their heritage and the roar of friends and family clapping, ululating, and cheering.

Dinner was a feast that crossed continents. Jollof rice, fried plantains, goat stew, pepper soup, alongside roasted vegetables, garlic mashed potatoes, and creamed greens. Sweet cornbread met puff-puff, and miniature pecan pies sat beside chin chin treats. The menu was a celebration of Southern and African palate tantalizing flavors, curated by a top Michelin chef. Guests also enjoyed southern dishes like shrimp and grits, collard greens with smoked turkey and plantain-stuffed chicken, paired with champagne, custom cocktails and mocktails. A sophisticated gourmet coffee bar was also featured.

The couple's wedding cake was a showstopper: a five-tier creation adorned with edible gold leaf, cascading sugar flowers, and a custom topper depicting the bride and groom in traditional African wedding attire. As Renee and David cut into it, the room erupted in cheers.

The live band was a highlight of the evening, blending smooth jazz, soul, and upbeat classics that got everyone on their feet. Throughout the evening, the couple incorporated meaningful elements that honored their heritage and personal journey with a small table displaying photos of loved ones who had passed, surrounded by candles and fresh flowers, ensuring their spirits were part of the day. Each guest received a small box containing items such as shea butter, artisanal gourmet chocolates, and a note from the couple expressing their gratitude.

Toasts, Secrets & Second Chances

The reception was in full swing—champagne bubbling, jazz pouring from a live band, and candlelight twinkling against the soft ivory drapery that wrapped the ballroom like a dream. Guests laughed, danced, and dined beneath golden chandeliers, surrounded by white roses and silver tableware that shimmered like moonlight. And then Monique tapped her glass. A soft chime silenced the room as she stood at the head table, wine glass in one hand, a mischievous smile tugging at her lips.

"I promise not to be long," she began, glancing toward the newlyweds. "But I do have a confession to make." Renee's brow lifted with suspicion. David tried—and failed—to stifle a grin.

"You all know I've been Renee's best friend since college," Monique continued, "which means I've seen every version of her—bedhead Renee, broken-hearted Renee, boss-lady Renee, and now…Mrs. David Bennett." The crowd chuckled, clapping lightly.

"But what you *don't know*," Monique said, pausing for dramatic effect, "is that this whole beautiful moment we're celebrating? This second chance at forever? It might not have happened if I didn't break into her drawer and steal a ring." Gasps and laughter rippled through the crowd. Renee's jaw dropped.

"*You didn't!*" Monique grinned unapologetically.

"Oh, but I did. While you were in the shower, boo. I snatched that ring out of the velvet pouch like a diamond thief in a rom-com. Slipped it to Romeo over here—" she pointed to David—"who then proposed under the stars like in a Hallmark Mahogany movie on steroids." Laughter exploded. David raised his glass, nodding toward her.

"Best accomplice I've ever had." Renee shook her head, laughing through tears.

"You really are the drama."

"I am," Monique said proudly. "But only for love." Then her tone softened. "In all seriousness though, watching you two find your way back to each other has been the greatest joy. Sometimes love doesn't look perfect the first time around. Sometimes it needs space, silence, and a few good friends willing to bend the rules." She lifted her glass high.

"To Renee and David—proof that the heart remembers, that time can heal, and that second chances…are sometimes the most beautiful beginnings."

"*To love!*" the crowd echoed, rising in a chorus of clinking glasses. David pulled Renee close, his lips brushing her temple.

"I knew she'd spill eventually," he whispered. Renee grinned.

"You both got lucky I didn't check that drawer."

"And I got even luckier," he murmured, "when you said yes." Monique raised a glass a second time with tears in her eyes and fire in her voice.

"To timing. To second chances. To soulmates who know how to *wait right*." Tasha followed up with laughter and sass.

"And to the man who finally pulled Renee out of her spreadsheets and into the arms of love!"

Later, Jackie gave a heartfelt toast, recalling childhood memories and praising the couple for their resilience. Malcolm also stood, his voice thick with emotion, as he expressed how honored he felt to walk Renee down the aisle. Then came the traditional wedding reception music. If the ceremony was sacred, the reception was soul. A jubilant gathering of heritage and high fashion, ancestral elegance and unfiltered celebration. The dance floor stayed packed all night, with guests of all ages joining in to celebrate love, life, and the beauty of togetherness. The band transitioned into a five-piece jazz ensemble, and the smooth sounds of Coltrane, Ella, and Miles filled the air. Couples swayed. Aunties hummed. Old friends reconnected over slow dances, stepping and whispering memories.

But soon enough, the energy shifted. A cousin grabbed the mic and announced what everyone had been waiting for: *"Y'all know what time it is!"* The DJ dropped *"Before I Let Go"* by Maze, and a spontaneous *Soul Train line* erupted right down the center of the tent. One by one, guests slid, stomped, twirled, and glided between the rows; heels off, dignity forgotten. Monique shimmied in a feathered dress. Tasha body-rolled like she'd rehearsed for a tour. Malcolm moonwalked backwards into cheers. Then David stepped in. He pulled Renee into the line and the tent exploded. They danced their way through, their movements smooth, their rhythm natural—as if the love between them had its own beat.

Line dances followed—*The Wobble, The Electric Slide, Cupid Shuffle, Tamia Line Dance,* and of course *Boots on The Ground*. Of course, being that it was held in North Carolina, there were fans everywhere. People came ready. There were hardly anyone seated during the line dances. Generations moving in sync, elders clapping and joining in, toddlers spinning on the sidelines, and that one uncle in snakeskin shoes and a fedora trying to challenge everyone to a dance-off, shuffling like James Brown.

And in the midst of it all, Renee stood still for just a second, letting the music wash over her. This—*this*—was what it felt like to be fully loved, fully rooted, and fully free. The evening was a whirlwind of laughter, dancing, and joy. The six bridesmaids made sure Renee barely sat down, pulling her onto the dance floor at every opportunity. David's friends did the same, and the couple's shared circles of family and friends mingled effortlessly.

As the night came to an end, the couple was sent off in grand style. Guests lined the courtyard, holding sparklers that lit up the night sky as the couple made their way to a classic black Rolls-Royce adorned with white roses and a chauffeur. Renee and David, hand in hand, walked through the sparkling tunnel, their faces illuminated by joy and the promise of their future. As they climbed into the classy vehicle adorned with a "Just Married" sign, David turned to Renee and whispered, "This time, forever." She smiled, her heart full.

"Forever," she agreed. And with that, they rode off into the night, ready to begin the next chapter of their love story with laughter, joy, and love in the air. Asheville's timeless charm and the couple's vibrant cultural celebration ensured this wedding would be remembered as a truly spectacular event.

The honeymoon suite was nothing short of an opulent sensual sanctuary. Tucked away in a private wing of an elite historic chateau-turned-resort, the room opened into a sweeping expanse of ivory and gold. A sybaris retreat, the room exuded intimacy and indulgence. A sweeping staircase led to a private loft, where a magnificent canopy poster bed stood elevated, as if resting on clouds. Below, the heart of the suite pulsed with romantic energy. Mirrored walls reflected the flickering candlelight and the steam rising from the in-room hot tub, casting a dreamy glow across the space. The tub, sunken and bubbling, sat beneath a constellation of soft lights, inviting them to soak in warmth and passion.

Every inch of the room had been curated for pleasure, for reconnection—for love. And here, David and Renee began their forever. The canopy bed was nestled on a loft with sheer curtains billowed in the gentle breeze from the balcony, as tall windows overlooked a moonlit garden, where rose petals floated in a fountain and soft music drifted from hidden speakers. Candles flickered everywhere—on mantels, windowsills, and surrounded the huge soaking tub near the fire, already drawn with lavender and milk bath oils. A tray of chocolate-dipped strawberries, champagne, and silk robes awaited them.

But David wasn't looking at the room. He was looking at her. Renee stood near the window in a floor-length sheer negligee of the softest cream, edged with lace that clung to her curves. Her hair was pinned just enough to fall freely when his hands removed them. Her eyes met his—full of trust, tenderness, and desire.

"This doesn't feel real," she whispered. David stepped toward her, his voice low.

"That's because it's finally right." He removed the hair pins to let her hair fall down to her shoulders and kissed her slowly, with the kind of reverence that rewrites memories. There was no urgency—only exploration. His hands traced her arms, her back, her waist like he was memorizing a song he planned to hum forever.

"You look like a dream," he whispered, brushing her cheek with the back of his hand.

"I feel like I never woke up from one," she replied, voice low and breathless. He guided her into the bed, parting the sheer curtains as if unveiling a secret. The world disappeared once they crossed that threshold. Within those veils, time slowed, as they relearned what they had once known so well—then lost—and now cherished even more.

They whispered memories and promises between kisses, their laughter tumbling between sheets and sighs. He paused more than once just to look at her, to brush a curl from her face, to remind her—again and again—that she was everything he ever needed. It wasn't rushed or hungry—it was a love ritual. A merging not just of bodies, but of years and forgiveness, of roads diverged and now made one. Wrapped beyond the sheer curtains, mirrors capturing fragments of their love from every angle, they made a new memory to eclipse the old. It was hours before they slept—tangled, peaceful, glowing. They made love under candlelight, tangled in silk sheets and soft moans, their movements slow and intentional, two hearts syncing after years of longing and healing. He kissed her scars. She touched his soul. And in every quiet gasp and whispered name, they promised to never let time steal from them again.

Later, with her curled into his chest and the fire casting shadows across the ceiling, David murmured against her hair.

"I didn't know a man could be this full." Renee smiled into his skin.

"Then let me overflow you."

The Morning After

The morning sun broke gently through sheer curtains, casting golden ribbons across the bed. Renee stirred first, her fingers instinctively reaching for him—and finding his arms already around her. For so many years, she had imagined this—waking up beside him, tangled in the sheets, knowing that this time, he was hers forever. David's eyes fluttered open, and he smiled, still husky from sleep.

"Morning, Mrs. Bennett."

"Mm," she hummed, eyes still closed. "Say it again." He kissed her shoulder.

"*Mrs.* Bennett." He brushed a kiss against her forehead.

"Last night was perfect."

"It was," she agreed. "You were perfect." David tucked a strand of hair behind her ear.

"I plan on making every night just as memorable." She sighed happily, melting into him.

"I can't wait."

A knock came at the door—soft and rhythmic. Moments later, a server rolled in a breakfast cart piled high with warm croissants, fluffy eggs, smoked salmon, fresh berries, and honey-drenched pastries. There was chilled juice, French-pressed coffee, and a single white orchid in a crystal vase. David signed the bill, tipped generously, and locked the door behind the server. Renee sat up, wrapped up in the bed sheets, nibbling on a croissant.

"Do we really have to leave this sybaris today?"

"We've got a flight to Paris, remember?" She sighed dreamily.

"Fine. But I'm packing the silk robes and your last name," she said jokingly. He laughed, climbing back into bed and pulling the tray between them. They fed each other strawberries, sipped coffee between kisses, and laughed at the tiny crumbs she left on his chest. Then, just as she was about to reach for the raspberry jam, he leaned in, eyes darkening slightly.

"One more round?" he whispered, voice low and inviting. Her grin was slow and delicious.

"I thought you'd never ask."

The honeymoon suite had been a dream, but now, they were about to step into another. As they arrived at the airport, David wrapped an arm around Renee's waist, pulling her close as they waited to board their private jet. "Paris, a city for lovers," he murmured in her ear. "How fitting." Renee smiled up at him.

"As long as I'm with you, anywhere feels like the city of love." David kissed her temple.

"Just wait. I have a few surprises planned." Her eyes lit up with curiosity.

"Oh? Should I be worried?" He smirked.

"Not at all. Just be ready to fall in love with Paris…and with me all over again."

As they walked hand in hand toward the stairs of the jet, Renee felt a wave of gratitude wash over her. Five years ago, she had let him go. Now, she was walking into "happily ever after" with him. And this was only the beginning. The hum of the engines was low and steady as the private jet soared above the clouds, slicing through the sky en route to Paris. The cabin, lavish and serene, was outfitted with plush cream leather, gold accents, and panoramic windows that framed the heavens like art. But David and Renee barely noticed. They sat side by side at first, fingers laced, legs brushing. The wait staff offered them a curated brunch spread; chilled mimosas, delicate pastries, and truffle-laced omelets, but neither of them had much of an appetite. Their hunger was of a different kind. Renee leaned into him, her lips brushing his earlobe. "How long until we're alone?" David smirked, already on his feet, pulling her gently toward the private suite tucked behind a sliding door at the rear of the jet. It wasn't large, but it was opulent—mood lighting, a queen-sized bed with silk bedding, and just enough space for two people who had no desire to be apart. The door clicked shut behind them.

They didn't bother undressing slowly—there was no time for a grand ceremony. His lips found her neck, her collarbone, her pulse. She clutched at him, tugging him closer, her silk blouse slipping from her shoulders as his hands traced the familiar curves of a woman he'd waited years to call his again. She laughed breathlessly as he backed her toward the bed, his eyes locked on hers like gravity had pulled him in for good. They made love with abandon—half a decade of longing, forgiveness, and rediscovered love crashing down like a tidal wave. The motion of the jet, the cocoon of clouds outside, the muted clink of glasses from the main cabin—it all disappeared as they moved together with a rhythm that belonged only to them. They emerged from the private suite briefly, flushed and glowing, accepting water and a fruit plate with sheepish grins—then disappeared again just as quickly for another rendezvous, the flight crew exchanging knowing smiles.

By the time the jet touched down on the runway in Paris, neither David nor Renee had touched their champagne. But their lips had never left each other. After the long ride from the airport, Renee stepped onto the private balcony of their suite, her breath catching at the breathtaking view of the Eiffel Tower shimmering under the night sky. Paris was everything she had imagined: romantic, timeless, enchanting. David appeared behind her, wrapping his arms around her waist, pressing a kiss to her shoulder.

"What do you think?" She leaned into him, sighing happily.

"It's perfect. Just like you." He chuckled.

"Well, the surprises are just beginning." David led Renee to a secluded spot in the Champ de Mars park, just beneath the Eiffel Tower, where a beautifully arranged picnic awaited; champagne, finger sandwiches, truffles and a cozy blanket spread out under the stars. The Eiffel Tower sparkled above them, illuminating the night with golden light.

"Did you plan this?" Renee asked, her voice filled with awe. David shrugged with a teasing smirk.

"Maybe I had a little help." She laughed, snuggling beside him as they toasted with champagne.

"This is a dream." David brushed a curl from her cheek.

"No, this is our reality. You, me, here, now." As he leaned in to kiss her, the lights of the Eiffel Tower twinkled, as if the city itself was celebrating their love.

The next afternoon, David took Renee on a romantic stroll along the Seine River. As they reached the historic Pont des Arts, the iconic love-lock bridge, she gasped when she saw a small, elegant envelope tied with a red ribbon hanging from the bridge's railing. David untied it and handed it to her. "Open it." Inside was a handwritten love letter, his words pouring out all the love and devotion he felt for her. *"For five years, I loved you from a distance, hoping one day you'd find your way back to me. Now that you're mine again, I promise to never let you go. You are my forever."* Tears welled in her eyes.

"Oh David…" He pulled out a custom lock with their initials engraved on it.

"Let's lock our love here, where millions before us have done the same." She nodded, overwhelmed with love, and together they fastened the lock to the bridge, tossing the key into the Seine, sealing their forever.

That evening, both dressed up in their finest glamour. David guided Renee through a narrow Parisian alleyway, leading her into a secluded courtyard draped in fairy lights. A violinist played softly in the background, and a single table was set for two, surrounded by candlelight and fresh roses at a hidden courtyard restaurant in Montmartre.

"David," she breathed. "This is incredible." He pulled out her chair, grinning.

"I wanted our first dinner as husband and wife in Paris to be unforgettable." They dined on exquisite French cuisine, laughing, reminiscing, and falling deeper in love. As dessert was served—crème brûlée with their names dusted in chocolate—David reached for her hand.

"To forever," he whispered. Renee clinked her glass against his.

"To us."

For the final surprise, David took Renee on a private boat ride along the Seine, the Parisian skyline glowing under the moonlight. The boat was adorned with roses and soft golden lanterns, making it feel like a fairytale. Soft music played, and David extended a hand.

"Dance with me?" Renee laughed, placing her hand in his. "There's no dance floor, silly."

"There is when I'm with you." As they swayed to the music, lost in each other, the city of love surrounded them, but nothing in the world mattered more than the man holding her close.

Hand in hand, they stroll through Saint-Germain-des-Prés the following day. Renee admires a vintage dress in a boutique window, and before she can blink, David's inside buying it for her. They share a kiss in the fitting room as she twirls in lace. While exploring an outdoor market, a local artist offers to sketch them. They sit posed, stealing glances and stifled giggles as he captures their joy. They walk away with the sketch, signed *Amour Éternel*—eternal love.

"You keep outdoing yourself," Renee whispered against his lips. David smirked.

"Get used to it. Loving you is my favorite thing in the world."

8

Building the Foundation

The airport traffic was bustling, the magic of Paris still clinging to their skin like a second perfume. But when David unlocked the front door and carried Renee across the threshold, the hush of home wrapped around them like a well-worn blanket. Everything was familiar— the soft gray walls, the scent of vanilla from the diffuser, the framed memories they'd both removed after their breakup, now proudly rehung. Yet nothing felt quite the same. The brownstone didn't echo anymore. It pulsed with warmth. It was their home.

Their suitcases remained by the door for days, half-open and ignored. They took their time settling in, more interested in slow mornings than unpacking. David cooked breakfast in nothing but pajama pants, and Renee danced barefoot to the coffee pot in his old shirts. They argued playfully over how many throw pillows belonged on the bed, and whether the guest room should be painted sage or cream. Love wasn't always grand gestures now. Sometimes it was post-it notes with silly doodles. Sometimes it was folding laundry side by side, or falling asleep on the couch mid-movie, limbs tangled like ivy. He'd brush her hair back while she read on the porch. She'd leave his favorite bourbon chocolates in his office desk drawer before a long workday. They still got dressed up for Friday night dinner dates, even if it was just at the bistro down the block. And still attended most Carrington family dinner nights. And on rainy days, they'd light candles and replay Paris playlists while she made tea and he whispered "Encore?" like they were still living out their honeymoon.

They started dreaming out loud—about a garden in the spring. A photo wall of their travels. A trip to the coast, just the two of them, no schedule, no phones. Sometimes Renee would catch herself pausing in the hallway, hand resting over her heart, marveling at how full it all felt. The second chance. The softness. The way love had returned not as a thunderstorm, but as gentle, steady rain that watered the roots of something lasting. And David? He never stopped watching her like she was a living poem—one he never got tired of reading aloud.

One year into their dreamlike wedding, Renee and David Bennett returned home from a year of off-and-on traveling around the world. They had explored cobblestone streets in Europe, cruised along turquoise waters in the warm Caribbean, and marveled at the wonders of the Serengeti. The second year had been everything they'd hoped for—an adventure of reconnection, laughter, and love. But now, their greatest adventure yet was just beginning.

The office walls of the Bennett Foundation were lined with photographs—not of the couple who ran it, but of the lives they'd touched. Smiling children, community events, scholarship winners, renovated shelters. Every frame told a story, and every story had been shaped by the vision of David and Renee Bennett. Three years had passed since they'd stood at the altar, and still, every day felt like an affirmation of that "I do." The foundation was their shared heartbeat—born of his passion and her brilliance, nurtured with late-night brainstorms, matching coffee mugs, and planned retreats that often turned into romantic getaways.

Renee had walked away from her prestigious corporate position two years into their marriage. The late nights, the boardroom battles, the burnout—it had once defined her, but now it was behind her. In its place, she found joy in something far more meaningful: waking up beside her husband with no alarm, crafting initiatives that mattered, and building a legacy together—not just of love, but of impact. Their days no longer revolved around deadlines and directors—they flowed on their own terms. Sometimes their meetings took place over croissants on the patio. Other times they skipped town entirely, disappearing to Tuscany or Cape Town, laptops in tow but often forgotten. Their office had no rigid schedule. Just heart.

And their love? Still fiery. Still insatiable. Still theirs. They'd kiss like teenagers in the brownstone hallway, whisper naughty things during Zoom calls, sneak away to their bedroom suite above the foundation headquarters for midday rendezvous. The mirrored walls of Paris had long been replaced with sunlit windows and minimalist decor, but the fire never dimmed. They answered to no one. They belonged to each other. Every project they funded, every soul they uplifted—it was done hand-in-hand. Their legacy wasn't just in the foundation's name, it was in the way Renee would look at David during a board meeting, or how he'd touch the small of her back when guiding her into the fundraising galas.

Their life was full, yet never frantic. Purposeful, but never burdensome. They had built something far greater than either could've imagined when they first fell in love; freedom, passion, and a mission rooted in grace.

And whenever they traveled now—be it to a mountaintop
resort or a quiet vineyard—they always brought two
things: their passports and their passion. Because for the
Bennetts, love had never been confined to a honeymoon.
It had simply been the beginning.

It was a quiet Saturday morning, the kind they had
started to cherish. No meetings, no calls—just
mismatched mugs of coffee, bare feet on hardwood floors,
and the scent of cinnamon waffles drifting through the
kitchen. Renee had woken up earlier than usual. She
couldn't sleep—not because of discomfort, but because of
the secret resting quietly inside her. She had taken the test
three times that week. All positive. All unbelievable. She
wanted the moment to be more than just *"surprise, we're
pregnant!"*. She wanted it to be *this is ours.* She had to be
creative.

Renee stood in the kitchen that sunny morning,
staring at the positive pregnancy tests in her trembling
hands. She hadn't been feeling herself lately, and now she
understood why. When David walked in moments later,
his face instantly concerned at her wide eyes, she

whispered, "Open the envelope on the table." Inside the envelope was a black and white ultrasound photo—still grainy and small, but unmistakable. There, in the curve of light, was the beginning of their next great adventure. David froze. For a heartbeat, he said nothing. Then his eyes lifted, wide, disbelieving, wet.

"Renee…" he breathed. "Are you serious?" She nodded, voice thick with emotion.

"We're going to be parents. We're having a baby. Well—*babies*." His breath caught.

"Twins?" She bit her lip and smiled.

"Two. Two little heartbeats. I heard them." David's joy was instantaneous. He swept her into his arms, spinning her around as they both laughed and cried.

"This is the best news babe," he said, his voice filled with wonder. He kissed her forehead. Her cheeks. Her lips. His voice cracked.

"You just made me the luckiest man alive. Again."

They stayed like that for a while—foreheads touching, hands resting over her still-flat stomach, hearts already fuller than they'd ever been. Outside, the world went on as normal. But inside? A new chapter had begun.

David's POV

I thought I knew what love was. I thought I'd already seen Renee at her most beautiful—dancing in Paris, glowing in candlelight, laughing with her head tilted back in our kitchen, cheeks warm with wine. But nothing, *nothing*, could've prepared me for the way I saw her that day. The day our sons were born. It started just before sunrise. Renee nudged me awake with a whisper, "David… I think it's time." Her voice was calm, but her eyes—wide, luminous—were full of something between excitement and fear. I jumped out of bed like a man who'd trained for this his whole life but forgot the playbook the second the whistle blew. Bags by the door, check. Car seats installed, check. Breathe? Not so much. She winced with a contraction as I helped her into the car, and I'll never forget the way she gripped my hand. Fierce. Focused. My wife, the warrior.

The drive to the hospital was quiet except for the rhythmic breathing Renee had practiced and my heart trying to punch through my chest. I kept one hand on the wheel and the other stretched across the center console, holding hers like it was the only thing keeping me tethered to Earth. Once we got there, everything moved in fast-forward and slow motion all at once. Nurses. Monitors. Gowns. Beeping. And Renee—stronger than I've ever seen her—breathing through it, eyes on me, steady as stone. And then it happened. She looked like a goddess. Tired. Tear-streaked. Glowing. And mine. In that room, under fluorescent lights and surrounded by nurses and monitors, time stopped. I saw life enter the world. I saw the woman I love become a mother—not just to one, but to two. And she did it with courage that left me in awe. She'll always be the love of my life. But that day? She became my hero.

The hospital room was dimly lit, soft jazz playing from David's phone speaker in the corner, one of Renee's favorite songs, the same one they danced to in Paris under the glow of the Eiffel Tower. But this night was not about memory. It was about legacy. Renee gripped David's hand tightly, her forehead glistening with sweat, her body trembling with effort and determination. And through it all, David never let go. He was her rock—steady, calm, patient. He whispered to her through every contraction, pressed cooled cloths to her face, kissed her temple, and told her how proud he was, how powerful she was, and how much he loved her. Despite the controlled chaos, David Bennett was a picture of calm, his steady presence like an anchor for Renee as she prepared to bring their twin boys into the world. David stood beside Renee, his warm brown eyes locked on hers, his strong loving hand wrapped securely around hers. He had never been more in awe of her—her strength, her determination, her ability to endure. He gently wiped the sweat from her brow with a damp cloth, his touch tender and deliberate.

"You're doing amazing, Renee," he said, his voice low and soothing. "Just focus on your breathing. I'm right here with you, baby." Whenever she winced in pain, he didn't flinch or show fear. Instead, he let her squeeze his hand, offering silent reassurance.

"We've got this," he whispered, leaning close so she could feel his presence. "Just think of Liam and Noah—they'll be here soon."

The delivery room was a whirlwind of activity, the hum of monitors and the efficient movements of the medical staff creating an atmosphere of urgency and focus. When the doctor announced that it was time to push, David didn't hesitate to be fully engaged. He maintained eye contact with Renee, encouraging her with every effort.

"One step closer, babe. You're incredible. I'm so proud of you." At moments when Renee felt overwhelmed, David grounded her with his calmness. He didn't speak unless it was to reassure her, letting her know she wasn't alone. Even when he felt his own emotions welling up—fear, excitement, and anticipation—he stayed composed, channeling everything into being her rock.

"You're finally there, baby," he whispered, his voice a balm. "I see his head…he's almost here. Push baby." With one last push and a cry that felt like both triumph and surrender, their first son came into the world.

"Liam," Renee gasped, her voice cracking. David's eyes welled as he watched the nurse lift the tiny, perfect boy into the air. Tears spilled freely as the first cries rang out— a sound more beautiful than any music he'd ever heard. He cut the cord with trembling hands, overwhelmed, whispering his son's name like a prayer.

"Liam," he said softly. "Welcome, little man."

But there was no time to lose himself in emotion—not yet. Moments later, another wave came, and Renee—though exhausted—found strength again. David coached her through the next round, his voice soothing and full of reverence.

"I see little Noah's head…he's coming. One more good push honey." She bore down, pain and grace blending into power, and with one final push, their second miracle arrived.

"Noah," David said through tears. "Oh my God…Noah." Two sons. Two perfect hearts. Liam was placed in Renee's arms first, and then Noah was tucked against her chest. Her tears flowed freely, joy and exhaustion woven into every breath she took. David knelt beside the bed, one arm wrapped protectively around all three of them, his forehead resting against hers.

"You are my hero," he whispered, his voice breaking. "I've never seen anything more beautiful or more incredible than what I saw tonight. You gave me our sons. Our family." Renee looked down at the twin boys, nestled against her, their skin so soft, their cries softening into sleepy coos.

"They're everything," she whispered. "We're everything." And in that quiet moment—beneath the glow of sterile lights and the warmth of love—David knew that this…this was the greatest chapter yet. He kissed her forehead.

"You did it, Renee," he said, his voice full of awe as he held her hand while the staff tended to her and his babies.

As the delivery room settled, and the medical team completed their tasks, David sat beside Renee, one arm protectively around her, the other holding their newborn son, Noah as Renee held Liam. The four of them together felt like the culmination of every hope, every dream. "You're a superhero," David whispered to Renee, pressing a kiss to her temple. "Our boys are perfect, just like you." Renee looked up at him, her exhaustion fading in the glow of his love and gratitude.

"I couldn't have done it without you," she said softly. In that moment, David's calm strength and unshakable love created a memory they would cherish forever—a testament to his unwavering presence in the most important moments of their lives.

Once home, in the quiet hours of those first nights, Renee found herself awake, watching the twins sleep. It was in those moments that she realized her priorities had changed. Her sons were her world, and she wanted to be there for every milestone. Working from home was flexible and fulfilling and allowed her to balance her work with raising Liam and Noah. Her home office became her sanctuary. While the twins napped, she worked on fundraising projects and connecting with clients over video calls. In the evenings, she and David took turns with bathtime, feedings and lullabies.

The early days were a blur of feedings, naps, diaper changes, and love—but perhaps the most demanding part of all was feeding two babies from one body. Renee had prepared herself, of course—books, lactation consults, a nursing pillow the size of a couch cushion—but nothing truly prepares a woman for the moment she has one hungry newborn in each arm and no sleep behind her.

From the start, Renee knew she'd need to be flexible. Liam had taken to breastfeeding easily—strong latch, always eager. Noah, more sensitive, needed a gentler approach. Rather than trying to tandem feed in those bleary hours of the night when her arms ached and her body begged for rest, Renee and David created a rhythm that worked for them. While she breastfed one twin, David would sit beside her—barefoot and devoted— bottle feeding the other with expressed milk she had pumped earlier. They would switch for the next feeding so that both boys got the benefits of her milk and the closeness of both parents.

"Tag team," David would whisper, handing her a fresh burp cloth like he was her right-hand man on the court.

Renee pumped between feeds, sometimes in the stillness of early morning while the boys dozed, sometimes with her head on David's shoulder as he rubbed slow circles on her back. The whir of the pump became the background soundtrack of their early parenting days, along with soft baby grunts and lullabies playing low. At times, she doubted herself—when her body felt stretched thin or her supply dipped slightly from exhaustion—but David was always there. "You're incredible," he'd say, kissing her shoulder, taking a twin from her arms before she could even ask.
"You're feeding *two* human beings. That's nothing short of heroic."

Over time, they settled into a flow. Sometimes she tandem fed in the rocker, arms aching, eyes fluttering shut. There were days the house was chaotic; milk-stained shirts, burp cloths draped on every surface—but never a moment their boys went without nourishment or love. Together, she and David made it work—not perfectly, but beautifully.

One sunny afternoon, as Renee sat in the backyard with the 18-month-old twins on a blanket, she marveled at how much her life had changed. Liam was busy stacking colorful blocks, while Noah giggled as he tried to chase a butterfly. David, ever the doting father, was on the patio grilling lunch, sneaking loving glances at his family. Renee felt a deep sense of contentment. Life was no longer about climbing ladders or chasing promotions. It was about watching her sons grow, hearing their laughter, and sharing quiet moments with her husband. Their foundation thrived, but it never overshadowed their family. Their clients respected their boundaries, and Renee learned to find joy in the balance she had created.

One cozy evening, after tucking the boys into bed, Renee and David sat on the couch, sharing a glass of wine.

"Do you ever miss it?" David asked, referring to her old VP job. She shook her head, smiling.

"No. This is what I was meant for. You, Liam, Noah—this is my purpose now. Everything else is just a bonus." David kissed her hand, his eyes filled with admiration.

"You've built an incredible life for us, Renee." She leaned into him, the warmth of his love and the joy of their family wrapping around her like a blanket.

"We built it together."

In that moment, surrounded by love, Renee knew she had everything she'd ever wanted—and more. Their lake house was where they spent summers and school holidays with the boys swimming, fishing, playing board games and David bought a small boat for them to take short trips out into the lake on lazy afternoons. All future Bennett Christmases were spent at the family cabin in Asheville. Renee would arrive with armloads of presents for everyone in the family. She would bake and cook the holiday feast with her mom and Jackie and her cousins. They would do family Christmas crafts. Renee would lead in the karaoke sing along and facilitated the Soul Train lines with the kids. The laptops never leaving their home on family trips was the Bennett rule. Family always came first. No more scrooging. No more losing.

The End

A Letter from Renee

Dear Reader,

If you've made it to this point, then you know my story. You've seen the love I lost, the silence I let speak for me, and the ache of regret that followed me like a shadow. And now…you've seen what happens when grace gives you a second chance—and you're finally brave enough to take it.

When David asked me to marry him all those years ago, I let fear answer for me: fear of not being enough. Fear of change. Fear of letting someone truly love the parts of me I hadn't learned to love myself. So, I walked away from the very thing I wanted most. I told myself I needed time. That I was being wise. Independent. Focused. But truthfully? I was protecting myself from joy because I didn't feel worthy of it. And I've learned—*protecting yourself from joy is the most dangerous kind of self-sabotage there is.*

That's the heart of this story. That's what "***If You***

Scrooge, You Lose" really means. When you let pride, pain, or perfectionism rob you of presence—when you shut out the warmth because you're scared it won't last—you *lose* the moments that matter most. The people. The connections. The joy.

This isn't just a love story. It's a lesson in not letting your past harden you. A reminder that vulnerability isn't weakness—it's *the doorway to everything real*. I got a second chance. Not everyone does. So this is me, reaching out from the page, gently urging you not to wait like I did. Love deeply. Speak honestly. Say yes while the moment is warm in your hands. Because if you scrooge…you *do* lose. But if you dare to open your heart again? You just might win everything.

With love,

Renee Bennett

Author's Note

Dear Reader,

Thank you for taking this journey with Renee and David—two people who remind us that love isn't always about getting it right the first time. Sometimes, it's about having the courage to return, to try again, and to say the words we were once too afraid to speak. This story came from a simple truth: the holidays, for all their sparkle and joy, can also shine a harsh light on the things we've avoided. Love left behind. Dreams deferred. Regrets we wrap like gifts we never meant to give ourselves.

If You Scrooge, You Lose is more than a romantic title; it's a quiet warning and a bold invitation. A reminder that guarding our hearts too tightly can cost us what we long for most. And that choosing connection, vulnerability, and love, especially when it feels risky, is the bravest thing we can do. Whether you're rekindling an old flame, learning to love yourself, or stepping out of fear for the first time in a long time, I hope Renee's journey speaks to something tender inside you. And if this book gave you even a sliver of hope, or a gentle nudge toward forgiveness—of yourself or someone else—then it's done its work.

124

With heartfelt gratitude,

C.L. Holden

C. L. Holden writes love stories layered with heart, history, and humanity. Known for her deep character connections and emotionally rich storytelling, she brings powerful, passionate Black love to the page with grace and soul.

A published author of inspirational and Christian love stories, ***If You Scrooge, You Lose*** marks a bold and personal step into the world of second-chance romance. Still grounded in themes of purpose and divine timing, Holden weaves unforgettable journeys where love is

never lost—only waiting to be reclaimed. She believes
love doesn't always follow the rules. And sometimes, it
just needs a little more time.